Born to be Wild

Written by Timothy Williams
Based on a story by Paul Young
and a screenplay by John Bunzel and Paul Young

Willowisp Press®

Published by **Willowisp Press**®
a division of PAGES, Inc.
801 94th Avenue North, St. Petersburg, Florida 33702

Produced by Daniel Weiss Associates, Inc.
33 West 17th Street, New York, New York 10011
in association with Warner Bros: Worldwide Publishing
4000 Warner Boulevard, Burbank, California 91522

Printed in the United States of America

2 4 6 8 10 9 7 5 3 1

ONE

THE EARLY-MORNING SUN WAS BREAKING through the thick blanket of fog that hung over the African landscape. Deep in the lush rain forest, a family of gorillas was out scouting for breakfast. The mother and father, an impressive pair, searched the trees for fruit. Nearby, their child, a baby girl gorilla about four months old, played in the bushes.

The young gorilla caught sight of a flock of birds circling overhead. She arched her neck and watched them curiously. As they flew south toward the river basin, the young gorilla leapt to her feet and started following them on foot.

As the young gorilla loped through the underbrush, farther and farther away from her parents, she noticed a strange sound: a sound she had never heard before, a sound that signaled danger.

Up above, the birds suddenly scattered. They changed direction and flapped away, panicked by the strange sound, which seemed to be moving closer.

Sensing danger, the young gorilla stopped and looked around for her parents, but they were no longer in sight. She let out a yelp for her mother. Then she listened for a response. But all she could hear was that strange sound, which was moving closer and closer.

About two hundred yards away, the mother and father gorilla were frantically calling out for their missing child. The father rose up on his hind legs and went into full display, roaring and beating on his chest. But his calls were drowned out by the strange sound, which was all around them now.

Meanwhile, the young gorilla started running at full speed, trying to retrace her steps to the fruit trees. But the strange sound was right in front of her now. She looked up and saw a Jeep cutting through the brush just ahead of her, tearing out plants and kicking up dirt. Her path was suddenly cut off as the Jeep skidded to a halt. Four men carrying guns were on board.

The young gorilla stared at the sight in front of her, terrified. She had never seen a Jeep before. Or men. But instinctively she knew she was in real danger. She cried out for help as the men jumped off the Jeep and crept toward her.

She decided to turn and run. Surely she could outrun them, and then she'd locate her parents and they'd take her home, where she'd be safe once again. As the men edged closer the young gorilla dropped down on all fours and spun around to run. But now there were two more men on that side of her, too, and these men were spreading out a large net between them. The young gorilla froze in her tracks. She was surrounded. She let out a loud, desperate shriek as

4

the thick net dropped over her and engulfed her body. Then everything went dark.

San Francisco is a dense, man-made forest of concrete and steel. The city is home to over a million and a half people. Gus Charnley was one of them.

He paced anxiously, chomping on a thick cigar. He was in a dark corridor of the San Francisco International Airport, somewhere near the cargo terminal. Puffing away, he watched as a bespectacled veterinarian named Daryl stood in the shadows, unlocking a metal container.

Daryl slipped on a pair of rubber gloves, then opened the container. Inside was the young gorilla, cowering in the corner. She peeked out of the container, bug-eyed, panting wildly.

"It's okay," said Daryl in a soft, soothing tone. "Relax."

The young gorilla whimpered as Daryl reached in and took hold of her head. He peered into her frightened eyes with a flashlight. Then he put a stethoscope to her chest, listening to her pounding heartbeat.

"Come on, already!" barked Gus. "I ain't got all night."

"She seems healthy," said Daryl, removing the stethoscope.

"Good. Lock her back up, then," ordered Gus as he pulled a thick envelope from inside his jacket. He tossed it to a slimy-looking customs agent who was lurking in the shadows.

"Here's your pay," growled Gus.

The customs agent caught the envelope and ripped

into it greedily. "It better all be here," the agent hissed, counting a wad of twenty-dollar bills.

Gus didn't bother answering. The minute Daryl had the lid back on the container, Gus lifted it off the counter and carried it outside. His pickup truck was double-parked at the curb with the engine running.

Grunting from the weight, Gus dropped the container in the bed of the truck, then jumped behind the wheel and squealed away.

TWO

TWO YEARS LATER

FOURTEEN-YEAR-OLD RICK HELLER WAS DRIV-ing his mother's car well over the posted 55-mph speed limit. But that was because the cops were chasing him.

Rick stomped on the gas pedal, weaving his mom's Volvo through the slow-moving downtown traffic. He kept blaring the Volvo's horn, trying to warn drivers ahead that he was coming through. He didn't want anyone to get hurt; he just wanted to get away from the cops in the squad car. So far, he wasn't having much luck.

The cop behind the wheel of the squad car stayed right on Rick's tail, maneuvering expertly through the city streets, closing the gap between them.

His partner barked into the car radio. "This is unit fifty-three. We're in high-speed pursuit of a blue 1985 Volvo." Squinting, he tried to read the Volvo's plate number as it whipped through the city streets a half block ahead. "License is . . . uh . . . JPH686. Over."

The radio crackled back: "We copy, fifty-three. We're running a check."

*   *   *

Rick raced the Volvo through a red light, narrowly missing a head-on collision with a station wagon. He spun the wheel and skidded through the intersection. The police car was now right behind him, its siren blaring.

Rick hit the gas and jerked the wheel to the right as the next cross street approached. The Volvo fishtailed around the corner, almost skidding up onto the sidewalk. Rick managed to straighten out the car just in time, then glanced quickly in the rearview mirror. The police car was still right on his bumper.

"Damn! I didn't lose 'em!" he muttered. "Well, if at first you don't succeed . . ." His words trailed off as he hung a hard left into a tiny alley. Seconds later, the police car tore into the alley after him.

Rick's eyes suddenly went wide. Sitting in the alley directly ahead of him was a large Dumpster overflowing with garbage. Rick was about to hit it.

He slammed on the brakes with all his weight and the Volvo screeched to a halt, barely a foot away from the Dumpster.

Rick was in shock but he didn't have time to collect himself. In his mirror he could see the police car had stopped behind him and the cops were jumping out to come arrest him. Rick kicked open the car door and hit the ground running. He sprinted down the alley, arms pumping, as the cops raced after him.

"Stop, kid!" one of the cops ordered.

"Yeah, right," Rick yelled back over his shoulder.

Up ahead was a chain-link fence about fifteen feet high. On the other side of the fence was another alley.

Rick knew if he could just get over that fence, he'd lose them. They'd never be able to scale it. He tucked his chin and dove at the fence, then clambered up the chain link with ease. He was an expert at this. When he reached the top, he flopped himself over the fence.

Riiiiiip!

His shirt had gotten caught on the razor wire. Rick was stuck hanging on the fence, his arms and legs flailing helplessly. It was over and he knew it. He'd been caught.

The two cops arrived at the bottom of the fence, huffing and puffing. Rick flashed them his best smile, putting up a brave front.

"That was pretty good," he said. "You guys are getting faster."

When Rick's mom got the call from the police department telling her that her son had been arrested, she was already in a bad mood.

She worked at the California Research Center, which was located on the Berkeley campus of the University of California. Her job was researching animal behavior. She was in a rotten mood because the whole morning had been wasted trying to work with a very uncooperative subject: a young female gorilla.

"Yes, this is Margaret Heller," she said into the phone.

"Mrs. Heller, this is the police department. I'm afraid we have your son in custody."

Margaret hung her head. "Again?" she said wearily. "Okay, I'll be right there." Margaret hung up the phone and walked back to a giant chain-link cage that sat in the middle of the lab. It was twenty feet wide and just as long. Inside it was divided into two sections by a gate: a play area littered with stuffed animals and toys, and a sleeping area containing an old rubber tire covered with blankets.

Sitting in the cage was the young gorilla that had been taken from Africa two years earlier. She had matured dramatically and stood almost five feet tall.

Margaret knelt down to the gorilla's level and eyed her through the fence. "Maybe you'll be a little more cooperative when I get back. Yes?" As she said this she also used sign language to say the same thing.

The gorilla watched Margaret's hands intently. As soon as Margaret finished signing, the gorilla suddenly snatched up her water dish and heaved it at Margaret. It bounced off the fence, dousing Margaret with water.

Margaret stood up, wiping off her face. Then she signed to the gorilla, "I guess that means no."

An hour later, Margaret was leading her son out of the police station.

"Next time I'm not coming down here to get you out," she scolded. "I can't believe you were driving my car!"

"Hey, I was just practicing for my road test," said Rick.

"Your road test is two years away!" she shot back.

Rick shrugged. "What can I say? I'm an over-achiever."

His mother suddenly grabbed his arm and gave

him a stern look. "You're skating on thin ice, pal. If your father were here right now, you wouldn't—"

Rick flinched at the mention of his father. He had walked out on them two years earlier and they hadn't seen him since.

"Well, he's *not* here, is he?" Rick exploded, then yanked his arm free. He stormed out of the police station.

Margaret let out a deep sigh. She wasn't really angry at Rick. She knew he was in a lot of pain because his father had deserted them. She just wished she could do something to make Rick feel better. Unfortunately, she didn't know how to explain to her son that his father didn't want to be a father anymore.

THREE

MARGARET GAVE LONG AND SERIOUS THOUGHT to what Rick's punishment would be. Driving without a license and speeding were serious offenses, so she couldn't simply ground him. No, this time she had to do something more drastic.

She made Rick a janitor.

Every day after school he had to ride his bike straight to the animal research lab where Margaret worked. From four o'clock to six o'clock, Monday through Friday, he was to sweep, dust, mop, and scrub the entire lab from floor to ceiling.

On his first day, Margaret presented him with a bucket full of cleaning supplies. There were rubber gloves, scrub brushes, a broom, a mop, and lots of liquid cleaner.

And as if all that weren't bad enough, the responsibility of keeping the gorilla's cage clean was now Rick's!

"You expect me to clean up after that giant hairball?" he exclaimed, pointing to the gorilla.

"Please don't refer to her as a hairball, Rick. Her name is Katie," said Margaret as she moved to the cage. "And yes, I expect you to clean up after her."

Rick shook his head in disgust. "This is too much."

"Just make sure she's secured in her sleep area if you go into her play area, and vice versa," warned Margaret. "Don't ever go in the cage *with* her."

"You don't have to worry about *that*," Rick scoffed.

Margaret waved Rick over to the side of the cage. "Come and say hello to Katie."

Rick shook his head in amusement. "Sure, why not?" He dropped his mop and stepped up to the chain-link fence. To his amazement, Margaret started signing to the gorilla as she spoke.

"Katie, this is my son, Rick," she signed. "He's going to be working here now. Be nice, okay? He's a friend."

Katie watched Margaret making hand gestures, then responded by throwing one of her stuffed animals against the fence.

Rick was baffled. Why was his mom using sign language on a gorilla? As far as he knew, only people communicated with sign language. His grandmother had been deaf, and the whole family had learned sign language so they could communicate with her. But signing with a gorilla? That was nuts!

"Mom, I hate to burst your bubble," he said, holding back a laugh, "but that gorilla can't understand you."

"Yes, she can," Margaret insisted. "Katie is the focus of my research here. I'm trying to teach her to communicate with humans. She already has a big vocabulary. And I speak when I sign to her, so she understands a lot of spoken words, too."

This time Rick couldn't hold back his laughter. "An ape that reads sign language and understands words? That's crazy!"

"You think so?" Margaret asked. "Sign to Katie. Tell her to go to bed."

Rick rolled his eyes. He couldn't believe his mother was asking him to sign to a dumb old gorilla.

"Go on," his mom dared him. "You used to sign all the time with Grandma. Tell Katie to go to bed."

Rick sighed, then halfheartedly made the hand gestures at Katie, signing, "Go to bed."

The gorilla watched Rick's hands moving through the different positions. When he finished signing, she picked up another one of her stuffed toys and heaved it at Rick. It bounced off the fence and landed on the floor of the cage.

"See?" said Rick to his mother. "She's just a dumb animal."

Rick went back to get his mop. He dunked it into a pail of soapy water, then started to wipe down the floor.

"Rick!" his mother called. She was still standing at the fence, peering into Katie's cage. "Look!"

Rick stopped mopping and glanced inside the cage. Katie had gone into the sleeping area and curled up inside her rubber tire, pulling a blanket over her body. She had gone to bed!

Rick stared through the chain link at Katie, totally amazed.

Margaret smiled proudly. "What was it you called her? A dumb animal?"

The next day, Rick was busy cleaning all the windows in the lab when he noticed his mom performing an experiment with Katie.

Margaret sat outside the cage and dipped her finger into a jar of red paint. She reached through the chain link and dabbed a glob of paint onto Katie's forehead. Then Margaret held a small mirror up to the fence so Katie could see herself, paint splotch and all.

"Who is this?" Margaret asked Katie as she signed.

Katie just stared into the mirror.

"Katie, who is this in the mirror?" she asked again.

Rick couldn't help but watch. He was curious to see if the gorilla understood what his mom was signing. And besides, it sure beat washing windows.

"What are you doing?" Rick inquired as he abandoned his work and sat down beside his mom.

"This is a test for self-recognition," she answered. "If Katie tries to touch the paint on her forehead when she looks in the mirror, it means she understands she's looking at herself, not another animal."

Margaret put the mirror back in front of Katie's face again.

"Who is this, Katie?" she asked patiently.

Katie stared into the mirror. For a minute it looked like maybe she did understand. But then she suddenly snatched the mirror and threw it to the floor, smashing it.

"She sure likes to throw stuff," remarked Rick, getting up and grabbing a broom and dustpan.

Margaret slumped against the side of the cage. "What am I doing wrong? How do I get through to her?" she muttered to herself.

"Maybe you should make her a janitor too," Rick suggested as he swept up the broken glass.

Margaret managed to smile. "Maybe," she said, rubbing her weary eyes.

Later that afternoon, Margaret left to go to the campus library for a while. As soon as she was gone Rick decided it was time to take a break.

He tore off his rubber gloves and dashed down the hallway to a row of vending machines. He bought a bag of M&M's, then wandered back into the lab, munching on them.

Rick sat with his feet propped up on his mom's desk, eyeing all the computers and high-tech equipment that lined the wall. Another whole wall was taken up with a huge bookshelf filled with books about animal behavior.

Bored, Rick leaned his head back and starting throwing M&M's into the air, catching them in his mouth. After he had done that three or four times, Katie started hooting at him.

Rick looked over and saw Katie was pressed up against the cage with her arm reaching out toward him.

"You want one of these?" Rick asked, holding up his bag of M&M's.

Katie hooted at him again. This time it was more insistent.

Rick lobbed an M&M across the lab at Katie. She craned her neck, her eyes locked on the flying M&M as it whizzed toward her. She looked like a baseball player about to catch a pop fly.

As the M&M sailed into her cage, Katie stepped into its path and caught it in her mouth. Then she ran back to the edge of the cage and hooted at Rick again.

"They're tasty, huh?" Rick laughed, tossing her another one. Katie caught it in her mouth with ease. She gulped it down and then screeched with excitement, swinging her arms over her head.

Impressed, Rick got up and walked to the edge of the cage. "You're pretty good at that, Katie."

Suddenly, in a lightning-fast move, Katie reached through the fence and swiped her huge arm toward Rick, ripping the bag of M&M's out of his hand.

"Hey!" Rick shouted as he jumped back, startled.

Katie hurried to the far corner of the cage with the M&M's, hooting gleefully.

"I don't have any more money, hairball! Give those back!" yelled Rick.

Katie turned her back to Rick as she sniffed the M&M's eagerly. Then she dumped the entire contents of the bag into her mouth, all at once. She looked back at Rick while she chewed with her mouth open. Wide open.

"Gross," uttered Rick. "Can't you at least chew with your mouth closed?"

Katie screeched back at him, still chewing. Rick could have sworn she was smiling, which only made him more angry.

"You're not a gorilla," he hissed, "you're a pig!"

By the time six o'clock finally rolled around, Rick couldn't wait to get out of there. His arms ached from all the scrubbing, and he wanted to get home and relax.

He was almost done mopping out the play area of

Katie's cage. Katie was secured in her sleeping area, watching Rick finish up.

"I hate this stupid job," he grumbled sullenly.

Katie stood up and hooted at him.

Rick shot her an irritated look. "And I'm not too crazy about you either, you M&M thief." He wheeled the bucket out of Katie's cage and put it away next to a big sink in the corner of the lab.

"I'm done," he signed at Katie, "so you can have the other half of your cage back." Then he pulled a cable hanging from the ceiling, sliding open the fence separating the two halves of the cage.

Katie scurried into the play area and grabbed her favorite toy, a Viewmaster. She loved to look into the eyepiece and click through reel after reel of pictures.

"Ooh, I see you have big plans tonight," Rick chuckled. "Gonna curl up with the old Viewmaster, huh?"

Rick grabbed his jacket, anxious to leave before his mom returned from the library with another long list of chores for him. "So long, banana brain!" he called back over his shoulder as he rushed for the door. But then he stopped because he noticed Katie was signing something at him.

It was the same word, over and over, but Rick couldn't tell what it was. It had been a couple of years since his grandmother passed away, so his sign language was a little rusty.

Katie signed the word again, this time slowly and more emphatically. Rick had no idea what she was trying to say.

"Sorry," he said with a shrug. "I don't know what you want." He headed for the door again.

Katie barked at Rick, trying to get him to stop. He ignored her, so she grabbed her food dish and flung it against the fence. Chunks of food went flying all over the place. This made Rick stop in his tracks.

"Hey!" he hollered. "I just cleaned in there!"

Katie was jumping up and down, signing that same word over and over at Rick.

"Knock it off, fleabag!" he yelled. "I'm outta here!" He turned and headed for the door, wanting to get the heck out of there.

As he stalked past the sink he noticed something in it.

It was a water dish. It had the word *Katie* printed on the side.

Rick picked up the empty dish and held it out for Katie to see.

"Is this what you want? Water?" he asked.

Katie signed the word again. Over and over.

Rick filled up the dish and carried it over to the cage.

"Go to bed," he signed. "Go to your sleeping area so I can bring the dish in."

Katie didn't budge. She stood in the center of the play area, her eyes riveted to the dish of water in Rick's hand.

"C'mon, I can't go in there unless you're locked in the sleep area. Mom's orders, remember?" he signed.

Katie wouldn't budge. She just stood there, signing that same word over and over as she stared at the water dish.

19

Rick couldn't stand it any longer. "Aw, the heck with Mom's orders," he mumbled, opening the door to her cage and stepping cautiously inside.

"Now you behave," he warned Katie as he edged toward her, holding the dish in his outstretched hand. He was expecting Katie to snatch it out of his hands, but to his surprise, Katie did just the opposite.

She slowly approached, looking deep into Rick's eyes. Then she gingerly reached up and wrapped her fingers around the dish, gently taking it from Rick.

Rick stood there watching her drink. He was impressed.

FOUR

THAT NIGHT RICK ROOTED THROUGH HIS BED-
room closet, digging past his baseball equipment and
old toys, frantically searching for something.

He finally located what he had been looking for, a
book called *Sign Language Made Easy*. The book had
been a gift from his mother on his sixth birthday so
that he could learn sign language and communicate
with his grandmother.

Rick sat on his bed and cracked open the book. He
looked up the word *water*. To his amazement, the hand
gestures that signified the word *water* were exactly the
ones Katie had been making at him earlier.

That meant Katie really did know how to communicate
with humans! She had been thirsty and wanted Rick to
get her some water, so she'd asked for it by signing *water*.

Rick was excited at the prospect of being able to talk
to Katie using sign language. He stayed up most of the
night studying the book, teaching himself how to sign
again.

"Students, faculty members, and friends, my name is
Lacey Carr," began the young girl. She was standing on

the stage of the high-school auditorium, addressing the whole school.

Lacey Carr was one of the brightest girls Rick knew at Jefferson High. Her desk was three rows over from his in science class, and he'd noticed she always knew the answer to every question the teacher asked.

The students had been marched down to the auditorium to hear campaign speeches from the seven students involved in this year's school elections. Most of the kids in the audience couldn't care less who was elected, but they did like getting out of class.

"I'm running for class president," Lacey continued from the stage. Her voice was soft but firm. When she spoke, she wasn't nervous, like most of the other kids giving speeches. She was brave.

Rick was seated in the middle of the auditorium, surrounded by unruly students. Most of them were laughing and chatting and having spitball fights. Some others were dozing off or reading magazines. None of them had been paying attention to the speeches being given, including Rick. He had been idly drawing a portrait of Katie in his notebook—until it was Lacey's turn, that is.

As soon as she walked up to the podium and started her speech, bidding for the office of class president, Rick put his pencil down.

He couldn't take his eyes off her. There was something about Lacey Carr that Rick found hard to resist. He wasn't even sure what it was—he just knew he liked her.

Rick doubted that Lacey even knew he was alive. He

figured it probably had something to do with the fact that he never knew the answer to any of the questions their science teacher asked.

"If I'm elected as your class president, I won't be afraid to tackle the tough issues," promised Lacey. "Like dissecting animals, for example. Why should we keep cutting up frogs when we can use computer models?"

Lacey paused for a second, letting the students consider her idea. It was during these few seconds of silence that Bubba Trainer, a fat kid sitting next to Rick, let loose with a huge burp.

The whole audience burst into laughter, except for Rick. Quick as lightning, he reached over and smacked Bubba in the back of the head.

"Knock it off, jerkface!" Rick ordered.

"Party pooper," Bubba sneered. "Do you have a crush on her or something?"

Rick didn't bother answering. His attention was on Lacey. She was standing at the podium, waiting for the laughter to die down so she could continue her speech.

"I believe we have an obligation to stop senseless animal experimentation," she stated. "We have a duty to protect innocent, helpless animals. We have . . ."

Lacey's voice trailed off. She stared down at the front row, where Monte and Franklin, two guys Rick recognized from his history class, were chatting loudly.

"*Shut up!*" she screamed at the top of her lungs.

Monte and Franklin jumped in their seats, startled by Lacey's abrupt outburst. The auditorium was suddenly very quiet and everyone was staring at Lacey. She seemed pleased.

23

"I hope you will all vote for me on election day," she concluded calmly. "Thank you."

Lacey waited for applause, but there wasn't any. Undaunted, she turned and walked back to her seat.

Clap! Clap! Clap!

The sound of one person clapping echoed in the auditorium. Everyone, including Lacey, looked to see who the lone clapper was.

It was Rick. He stood up and continued clapping with earnest appreciation for her speech. No doubt about it—he had taken a real liking to Lacey Carr.

The rest of the week, whenever Rick was alone in the lab with Katie, he would immediately abandon his work and talk to Katie using sign language.

Rick wasn't sure why, but for some reason Katie was a lot more cooperative with him than she had ever been with his mom. Rick figured maybe it was because he and Katie had something in common: they both had lost their families. Katie had lost her family when she was taken out of Africa, and Rick had lost his family when his dad walked out.

Rick loved to sit at the edge of the cage and sign with Katie. He was still having a hard time signing, so he was slow and unsure when he did it. But Katie was a different story. Sign language was second nature to her, so she was able to make the hand gestures very quickly and very confidently.

Rick would sign simple things like, "Do you want to eat?"

She would sign back, "No, I want to play."

Rick would then ask her, "What do you want to play?"

She would sign back, "I want to play Viewmaster." Then she'd run into her play area and grab her Viewmaster. She'd stare into the eyepiece for hours, hooting merrily as she clicked through the picture reels.

One day Rick decided to teach her something he knew how to do. He got out some blank paper and his mom's finger paints and took them into her cage.

"Do you want to draw?" he signed.

Katie signed back, "What draw?"

"I'll teach you what drawing is," he said, opening the paint cans.

Rick dipped his finger into some paint. He then finger-painted a simplified outline of a bird on the paper. Finally he showed it to Katie.

"This is a bird," he signed. "Katie draw."

Katie dipped her finger into the paint, then promptly stuck it in her mouth. Rick grabbed her hand and yanked the finger out.

"No, no, it's not food!" he corrected her. "Bird, bird."

Katie had no idea what a bird was. The last time she had seen one was in the African rainforest, right before she was captured. But that had been two long years before.

"Bird. Bird," Rick signed as he drew another outline of a bird on the paper. "Now Katie draw."

Katie dipped her finger into the paint again. Rick watched her closely, ready to grab her hand again if necessary. But this time Katie placed her finger on the paper and drew a rough imitation of Rick's drawing.

Rick beamed proudly. "You did it," he signed, delighted. "You drew a bird! A pretty good one, too."

Katie threw back her head and hooted. She was having fun.

"You want to draw something else?" Rick signed.

She signed back, "Katie draw," before eagerly dunking her finger into the paint again.

But this time she didn't use paper. Instead, she reached over and drew the bird outline across the middle of Rick's forehead.

Rick laughed. "I didn't mean draw on me!"

Katie clapped excitedly.

"Okay, have it your way," he exclaimed, dunking his hand into a can of paint. Then he ran it across Katie's brow, leaving a yellow streak.

Katie loved it. In return, she attacked him with a handful of blue. Rick nailed her with a glob of green. Katie assailed him with purple.

Soon they were chasing each other around the cage, smearing paint on each other's faces. They were laughing and screaming and having a great time—right up until the second Margaret walked in.

"What in the world is going on here?" she demanded. She stood in the lab doorway with her mouth hanging open, staring at the sight in front of her.

Rick and Katie were in the cage, covered from head to toe with six different colors of paint. The walls and most of the floor were also heavily splattered with paint.

Rick and Katie froze when they saw her. Rick cleared his throat nervously.

"I was teaching her how to draw," he answered timidly.

Margaret exploded. "You're not supposed to be teaching her anything!" She tore open the cage door and yanked Rick out. "I'm the teacher here. You're just the janitor, remember?"

"All right," Rick said in a low voice. He knew he had gone too far. "I'm sorry."

Margaret grabbed a towel and went into the cage, stepping around the huge puddles of paint. She knelt in front of Katie and started wiping off her face. "This is serious research, Rick, not art class! There's a scientific program that has to be followed here!"

"Okay, okay!" he snapped as he turned on the sink faucet and started washing the paint from his face. "I said I was sorry. What more do you want from me?"

"I want you to get the mop and clean this mess up, on the double!" she ordered.

Rick dried his face, then reached for the mop.

"Hey, at least she was happy for a few minutes," Rick muttered under his breath. "That counts for something, doesn't it?"

FIVE

THE CHARNLEY FLEA MARKET WAS LOCATED IN a large warehouselike building in a run-down part of town. Gus Charnley had bought that particular building to house his flea market because it was cheap. It didn't bother him that it sat in such an undesirable location, or that it was downright ugly. He liked the fact that it was cheap. Gus hated throwing good money away for nothing.

Gus had a cheap sign posted outside the building that read *Charnley Flea Market—The Home of Bobo!*

The inside of the flea market was crammed with aisle after aisle of booths. Bargain hunters could shop for costume jewelry, sneakers, T-shirts, electronic gadgets, and tube socks. In the back sat a number of fast-food counters, where hot dogs, pizza, and doughnuts were available.

Next to the doughnut counter was a doorway that led to another, smaller room. A huge sign was plastered on the wall, pointing toward the doorway. It had a crude drawing of a fierce gorilla on it. The gorilla was baring its fangs.

This Way to Bobo!

On the other side of the doorway was a room with a tiny Plexiglas cage in it. The cage was decorated with Styrofoam rocks and fake plants. This was Bobo's home.

Bobo was a lowland gorilla, just like Katie. He was thirty-two years old and had lived most of his life in the tiny cage, with barely enough room to turn around. All day long shoppers would come in to stare and laugh and point fingers at him. It was a terrible life, and as a result Bobo's health suffered.

One morning Bobo collapsed, and Gus was forced to call Daryl the veterinarian. Gus hated to do that, because veterinarians cost a lot of money, but this time he had no choice. If he couldn't keep Bobo on display, he might lose customers. If he lost customers, he'd definitely lose money. And Gus hated losing money.

Daryl rushed over as soon as he got the call from Gus. When he arrived at the flea market, Bobo was weak and lethargic.

"His heart's in bad shape," reported Daryl. He was listening to Bobo's heartbeat with a stethoscope. "He should be in a facility where I can monitor him."

Gus didn't like hearing that at all.

"Are you out of your freakin' mind?" he bellowed at Daryl. "I'm running a business here!"

"I'm just telling you what's best for the animal," replied Daryl, gently stroking Bobo's head.

Gus barked, "What about what's best for me? How am I gonna make any money if he's in the hospital? Besides, Bobo likes it here." Gus reached out a hand to pet Bobo. "Don't you, boy?"

Bobo recoiled, hissing at Gus with obvious hatred.

Gus quickly pulled his hand away. "The gorilla stays," he said angrily. "We wouldn't want to disappoint the shoppers." Gus glared at Bobo, then walked out.

Daryl felt awful. He wanted to help Bobo, but there was nothing he could do, short of stealing him.

"I'm sorry, big fella," he whispered to the animal.

Bobo went limp in Daryl's arms. He looked up at Daryl with sad, tired eyes. He was a defeated animal, with no fight left in him.

As Daryl cradled the poor, abused animal in his arms, Bobo closed his eyes for the last time.

As soon as Gus heard the news of Bobo's death, he rushed over to the California Research Center, where his other lowland gorilla was being kept.

Two years earlier, when he had bought the young gorilla, he had worked out a deal with the research center. They had agreed to keep the young gorilla, feed her, and take care of her until Gus needed her. In exchange, the center would be able to do their valuable research on the animal.

The deal worked out well for everyone. Gus didn't have to pay for the gorilla's upkeep, and the lab had a subject for their research.

But now with Bobo gone, Gus needed someone to take his place in the Plexiglas cage. On his way to the research lab in his truck, he wondered if he'd have to pay for a new sign, or if he could just start calling Katie Bobo. He hated throwing money away.

*   *   *

"I came as soon as I got your message, Professor. What did you need to see me about?" Margaret asked as Professor Mallinson ushered her into his private office. When she entered the room, she was shocked to see Gus standing in the corner of the office, smoking a big fat cigar.

"What's he doing here?" she asked, scowling at Gus with obvious disdain. Margaret made no effort to hide her loathing for Gus. She had made it clear she didn't approve of the way he treated his animals.

Gus blew some cigar smoke in her direction. "I'm here for my property, Meg."

"My name is Margaret," she corrected him tersely.

"Whatever," Gus said with a shrug. "Now hand over my ape."

Margaret turned to her boss, Professor Mallinson. "What is this all about?"

Professor Mallinson sat behind his desk with a look of dread on his face. As the administrator of the research center, he was in charge. He had hired Margaret to teach Katie sign language in the hope that one day the gorilla would be able to communicate with humans.

"Something's come up," the professor said to a very angry Margaret. "Mr. Charnley needs his gorilla back."

"Now," Gus added. "Right now. Today. This ain't a social call."

Margaret snapped, "You can't have her!"

"Sure I can, Meg," Gus snapped right back. "I own her."

Margaret glared at him. "My name isn't Meg. It's Margaret. Better yet, why don't you just call me Mrs. Heller?"

"Hey, you're still using your married name, huh?" Gus sneered. "I thought you'd have changed it after your husband dumped you."

Now Margaret was steaming. She turned on Gus and got right in his face. "How dare you bring up my personal life, you . . . you . . ." she fumed.

"Now, now," Gus said soothingly, "don't get overheated, Meg."

"*It's Margaret!*" she yelled at the top of her lungs. "Not Meg, but Margaret!"

Gus blew a smoke ring at her. "Boy, getting dumped by your husband sure has made you cranky, Meg."

"Just get out of here," she ordered, pointing to the door.

"Not without my gorilla," he replied, waving his cigar at her.

Margaret turned to Professor Mallinson. "Sir, you can't let this man take Katie."

"What can I do, Margaret?" He shrugged helplessly. "Mr. Charnley owns her."

"But we have a lease on her!" she said sharply.

"You *did*," Gus said with a smirk as he took a copy of the lease out of his back pocket. "Indeed you did. But as luck would have it, your lease on my gorilla expired a week ago."

"That's impossible!" scoffed Margaret.

"He's right, Margaret," admitted Professor Mallinson. "I let it expire."

Margaret looked at the professor in shock. "But why? My research with Katie is far from over. You've got to renew, sir!"

Professor Mallinson shifted in his chair, then cleared his throat. Finally he said, "Margaret, look at the reality here. Katie isn't making any progress."

"So you want to get rid of her, just like that? And give her back to this creep?" she said, pointing a finger at Gus.

"Sticks and stones may break my bones, but names will never hurt me," said Gus merrily.

Margaret ignored him. She was too busy pleading with Professor Mallinson. "Please, sir. We can't stop our study now. Katie is starting to make progress! It's clear she has abstract memory. I think she even knows the difference between right and wrong!"

"I know *you* believe that, but do you have any hard evidence?" asked the professor.

"No," Margaret had to admit. "But I'm close. And if you let Mr. Charnley take Katie, all our work will go to waste."

Gus stepped closer, breathing cigar smoke on Margaret. "Look, Meg," he said, "I bought this gorilla to replace Bobo when the time came. That time has come."

"I'm afraid we have no choice," the professor admitted to Margaret. "We are only the caretakers for Katie. Mr. Charnley owns her."

Margaret felt as though her whole world was crashing down on top of her. She couldn't lose Katie, especially not to someone as mean and cruel as Gus.

"You can't take him!" she pleaded to Gus.

"I can and I will," stated Gus flatly. "If she's not packed and ready to go by the end of the day, I'll haul your butt into court." With that, Gus marched out of the office.

＊　　＊　　＊

"Where's Katie?" Rick demanded. "What have you done with her?"

Rick had gone to the lab after school, as usual. But when he got there, he discovered Katie's cage was empty and the lab was deserted. He raced home and found his mom lying in bed. Her eyes were red from crying.

"Why aren't you at the lab?" Margaret asked Rick. "It's only five o'clock. You're supposed to clean until six."

Rick glared at her. "Why aren't *you* at the lab?" he asked angrily. "You're supposed to be working with Katie, remember? But gee, I guess you can't, seeing as she's gone!"

"Rick, let me explain," she said sadly.

"Why did you get rid of her?" he spat. "It's because she doesn't like you, right? You're probably jealous because she likes me a lot more than she likes you!"

"Stop it!" she suddenly yelled, her voice breaking. "I didn't get rid of Katie. Her owner came and took her back."

"Who's her owner?" asked Rick.

Margaret shook her head. "Gus Charnley."

"The flea-market guy?" Rick asked, his face suddenly registering what that meant. "You mean . . . Katie's on display there?"

Margaret nodded weakly. "His old gorilla passed away, so he took Katie and . . ."

"And made her a sideshow attraction?" he finished for her.

"I feel just awful about it," Margaret said, a sob in her voice.

"Well, feeling bad isn't going to do any good, Mom. You gotta do something about it! You gotta get her back!" Rick insisted.

"I can't," she sadly informed him. "That man owns her, and there's nothing we can do about it."

"So you're just gonna give up?"

She looked at him with tears in her eyes. "I have no choice."

Rick threw up his hands in anger. "You're just gonna let her go! The same way you let Dad go! You didn't fight to keep him either!"

Margaret seemed suddenly angry. "You're skating on thin ice, mister. We better have a family talk about—" she started, but Rick suddenly interrupted her.

"What family?" he yelled. "We're not a family! It takes *three* to make a family!"

Margaret started to say something, but Rick turned and stormed out of the bedroom. He grabbed his jacket and raced out of the house, slamming the front door behind him.

SIX

RICK LOCKED UP HIS BIKE OUTSIDE CHARNLEY'S
Flea Market and ran through the front doors, frantically
pushing and shoving his way through the crowd of
shoppers, searching for Katie.

It wasn't long before he spotted the new sign on the
wall: *This Way to Katie!*

Rick found her locked inside the tiny Plexiglas cage.
A large group of shoppers had converged around the
cage and were staring at Charnley's newest attraction,
gawking and laughing and pointing.

Rick wanted to tell them all to shut up and get away
from the cage, but he knew that would only make matters worse.

He pushed his way to the front of the crowd and saw
Katie going berserk inside the cage. She was terrified,
screaming and shrieking at the top of her lungs. It
broke Rick's heart to see her like that.

Suddenly Katie recognized Rick and threw herself
against the side of the cage. She pawed at the
Plexiglas, trying to touch him. She was signing, "Out!
Out! Out!"

Rick signed back, "I want you out, too, Katie."

Katie signed desperately, "Out. Home. Katie go home."

Rick was near tears as he signed, "I know. I'm sorry."

"What in the world are you doing?" a voice asked from over Rick's shoulder.

Startled, Rick turned around to see whom the voice belonged to.

Lacey Carr was standing behind him. Rick stared at her, befuddled, with his mouth hanging open.

"That looked like sign language," noted Lacey, moving closer to Rick.

"It is." He gulped nervously.

"And you can use it to talk to him?" she asked, pointing at Katie.

Rick nodded. "Only he's a her," he stammered. "I mean, it's a her. I mean, she's a girl."

"I get the picture," Katie responded. "Who taught you sign language?"

"My mom," answered Rick. "She's a she, too," he said, joking to cover up his nervousness.

"Cute," said Lacey sarcastically. "So, did your mom teach the gorilla sign language, too?"

"Yeah," replied Rick, turning his attention back to Katie. "But that was before some slimeball stuck her in this cruddy little prison."

Lacey moved closer to the cage, studying Katie's frightened face.

"She looks awfully scared," Lacey said with a frown. "And sad."

"She doesn't like being in there," Rick said angrily. "She's not used to a bunch of people gawking at her like she's some kind of freak."

Lacey must have heard the concern in Rick's voice, because she looked over at him now, studying his face.

"You look sad, too," she said.

Rick could only nod. Then he turned his attention back to Katie, who was still signing, "Out! Out!" After that she began another series of signs.

"What is she saying to you?" Lacey asked.

"She's asking me to get her out of there. She's cold and hungry and thirsty and scared."

"Wow," Lacey exclaimed. "She can say all that?"

"She's real smart," Rick replied as he signed back to Katie through the Plexiglas.

"What are you telling her?" Lacey asked, watching Rick's hand gestures.

"I'm telling her that I'm not going to let her stay in there. I'm telling her that I'm going to get her out of there."

"But how?" Lacey wanted to know. "How can you do that?"

Rick shook his head. "I don't know yet."

The crowd was growing. More and more people were huddling around Katie's cage, anxious to get a look at her. Some of them made faces at her. Others rapped on the Plexiglas.

Katie was scared to death. She looked at Rick, her eyes pleading for help.

"Out! Out! Out!" she signed to him, over and over.

"Lacey, are you in there?" a man's voice called from the doorway.

"Uh-oh," said Lacey, peering back through the crowd.

"That's my father. He came here to buy a few things—socks, toothpaste, and car wax. Guess he's finished his shopping spree. That means I have to go."

Rick and Lacey shared an awkward look. Neither one of them knew what to say at that moment. Rick was secretly wishing Lacey would stay with him, but he didn't know how to say it to her. And he had the idea that Lacey didn't want to leave him, either.

"I'm sorry about your gorilla friend," she said finally, breaking the awkward silence between them. "You know how I feel about animals being abused like this."

"Yeah," said Rick. "I remember your speech at school the other day."

Lacey looked down at the floor, embarrassed. "You're probably the only kid in school who does. Nobody else was listening."

Rick leaned over until he was in her line of vision. "Hey, it wasn't your fault. It was a good speech."

"Thanks," she said, managing to smile. "By the way, thanks for clapping for me." She looked across the room again. "My dad's checking his watch—I guess he's getting impatient. So I better go," she said to Rick. "But if I can do anything to help, just let me know."

"I will," replied Rick. "Thanks."

Rick leaned against the side of the cage, trying to comfort the gorilla. Suddenly he turned around and saw Lacey, who had taken only a few steps and was standing there looking at him. As he watched she shook her head sadly and then stalked over to where her father was waiting. His arms were full of packages from the flea market.

"Daddy, how can you shop here?" Rick heard her say. "This place is horrible!"

Rick stayed at Katie's side the rest of the afternoon. There was no way he was going to desert her. He hung out at the side of the cage, signing back and forth with her, until an hour before closing time.

"I have to go, but I'll be back soon to get you out," he signed.

"Katie out! Out! Out!" she signed back desperately.

"Yes, Katie out! Soon!" he signed to her.

"No leave Katie!" she signed. "No leave Katie! Katie go with Rick!"

"Rick come back for Katie soon," he signed.

"Katie out now!" she signed.

It broke Rick's heart, but he had to leave her. "No!" he signed. "Katie out soon! Promise!"

Katie slumped against the Plexiglas, despondent.

"Katie be good," signed Rick. Then he quickly turned and ran out of the flea market. He hated leaving her there more than anything, but he had to because it was the only way to put his plan into motion.

Rick jumped back on his bike and went over to the research center. When he got there, the lab was deserted.

Working fast, he grabbed his sign language book and Katie's Viewmaster, then raided the toolbox, taking a pair of bolt cutters. He threw everything into a burlap bag and started out.

Then a sudden idea stopped him in his tracks. He went back to his mother's desk and fished through the drawers until he found a small key ring labeled *Van*.

Rick grinned. "Yeah," he said out loud. "I'm tired of riding my bike." He pocketed the keys and ran out to the parking lot.

Rick drove the research lab's van back to the flea market and parked outside. Clutching the burlap bag under his arm, he went inside and walked up and down the aisles, looking for a good hiding spot.

He finally decided the men's room would be the best place. He went in and locked himself inside a stall, then crouched on the toilet so the stall would look empty.

About half an hour later, the lights blinked off and on and Rick could hear the shoppers leaving.

A few minutes after that, a uniformed security guard poked his head inside the men's room. He took a quick look at the floor underneath the stalls, looking for feet. There weren't any.

"Anybody in here?" he called out. "It's closing time."

Rick held his breath, afraid to move a muscle.

The guard went out, shutting the door behind him.

"So far so good," Rick whispered to himself.

He crept silently out of the stall and cracked open the bathroom door.

Across the flea market, Rick could see the guard locking the front door. Once it was secured, he reached up and unrolled a large metal gate from the ceiling. It clanked to the floor and he locked it in place.

His work done for the night, the guard sauntered into a back room, twirling his keys on his fingers as he hummed to himself. Then most of the lights went out.

Rick opened the bathroom door a little bit wider and looked around. The flea market was dark and deserted.

Overhead, a surveillance camera was mounted near the ceiling. It slowly swiveled from side to side. Rick waited until it was pointed the other way, then dashed out of the men's room. He snuck down a darkened aisle past a huge display of cheesy sunglasses, turned a corner, crept past the fast-food counters, then ducked through the doorway that led to Katie.

Rick found the gorilla curled up in the corner of the Plexiglas cage, shivering, unable to sleep. She looked tired and haggard—until she caught sight of Rick sneaking into the room. The instant she saw him she jumped to her feet, hooting urgently.

"Out! Out!" she signed.

"That's the plan," Rick murmured with a smile, taking out the bolt cutters and going to work on the cage's padlock.

Snap!

He cut the lock off and ripped the lid open. In a flash, Katie shot out of the cage, knocking Rick off balance. He fell to the floor, landing on his face.

"Man, you're strong!" he said, breathless.

Katie was ecstatic. She beat her chest, hooting wildly and jumping around the room. She was so excited to be free!

"Let's get outta here!" whispered Rick as he climbed to his feet. He reached for Katie's hand so he could show her the way out, but she simply ran past him, bolting through the doorway.

"Wait! Katie, stop!"

It was too late. Katie was gone.

She raced through the flea market, knocking over anything in her path. Tube socks and T-shirts were spilled all over the place. Rick chased after her, knocking over his share of merchandise in the process, but he couldn't catch up to Katie. She was simply faster and a lot more agile.

The security guard was relaxing in the back room with his feet up. He was expecting this to be just another quiet night. But that all changed as he glanced at the surveillance monitor. On the screen he saw a gorilla and a kid racing through the flea market, making a heck of a mess.

The guard leapt out of his chair and raced into the flea market. He shone his flashlight around and spotted Katie. She was running right toward him, hooting and shrieking, her arms flapping wildly.

"Aaaaahhhhhh!" he cried, dropping his flashlight and running in the other direction.

Rick caught up to Katie and grabbed her hand.

"This way!" he panted. Together they sprinted to the exit, coming face-to-face with the huge metal gate that covered the door. They skidded to a halt.

"We're trapped!" said Rick. "Now what?"

Katie roared at the gate. She grabbed the barrier with both hands and started to shake it violently.

Rick watched, amazed, as the gate actually started to groan and twist from her efforts. With a final surge of Katie's brute strength, the gate popped out of the ceiling and fell to the floor in a tangled heap.

"Wow," was all the wide-eyed Rick could manage to say.

SEVEN

"AM I NUTS, OR WHAT?" RICK PONDERED ALOUD.
He was driving a stolen van with a stolen gorilla in the front seat next to him. He had no idea where to go or what to do next.

Rick ended up outside Lacey Carr's house. He figured if anybody knew where to hide a hot gorilla, it would be her.

Rick parked the van at the curb. Her house was dark, which meant everyone was probably in bed already.

"This is gonna be fun," he muttered sarcastically, fixing his hair in the rearview mirror. He knew that one of her parents would probably answer the door, and it was going to be tough to get past them this late at night.

"Stay," he signed as he climbed out of the van. "Stay here. Be good."

"Katie stay," she signed back. Then she jumped into the driver's seat and started looking through her Viewmaster.

Rick walked up to the Carrs' front porch, tucking in his shirt. He took a deep breath, then rang the bell. A

44

minute later the porch light snapped on and Lacey's father opened the door. He had pajamas and a bathrobe on, and was rubbing his face as if he'd just woken up.

"Oh boy," Rick sighed to himself, then plastered an innocent grin on his face.

"Good evening, Mr. Carr!" he chirped. "How are you this fine evening?"

Mr. Carr looked with obvious disdain at the kid standing on his porch.

"Are you selling something?" he asked, seemingly ready to slam the door in Rick's face.

"No sir!" Rick blurted through his smile. "I'm a friend of Lacey's. Is she in?"

"Yes, she's in!" Mr. Carr snapped. "She's in bed! Asleep!"

Rick had a hard time keeping the smile on his face, considering how poorly things were going with Mr. Carr. "I see," he said, struggling to maintain his grin. "Well, could you possibly wake her, sir?"

Mr. Carr's eyes narrowed. "No, I couldn't possibly wake her!" he bellowed. "Do you have any idea what time it is?"

Rick shrugged innocently. "Seven-thirty? Maybe eight?" he guessed.

"Try ten-forty-five, young man!" Mr. Carr snarled, holding out his watch as proof.

"Wow, nice watch," said Rick. "That's an excellent timepiece you have there, Mr. Carr. Was it a gift from your lovely wife?"

Mr. Carr had heard enough. He started to shut the door. "Good night, young man," he said gruffly.

Just in the nick of time, Lacey appeared at the top of the stairs, wearing sweats.

"Who is it, Daddy?" she inquired.

"It's Rick Heller, that's who!" Rick yelled through the crack in the door.

"Rick, what are you doing here?" she asked, coming to the door and stepping in front of her father.

"I have to talk to you," Rick said urgently. "It's real important!" He shot a look at Mr. Carr. "Big science test tomorrow. You know how it is."

But Mr. Carr didn't buy it. He pointed a bony finger at the staircase, glaring at his daughter.

"Upstairs, Lacey. Back to bed."

Lacey didn't budge. "Please, Daddy. Just five minutes." She turned her pretty blue eyes on her father, and he instantly crumbled.

"Okay . . . five minutes," he warned, tapping on his watch. "And then the weird kid goes."

Mr. Carr stalked down the hallway and disappeared into the kitchen. As soon as he was gone Lacey turned to Rick.

"What's going on?" she asked.

"Come outside," he insisted, taking her arm and leading her across the yard. "I gotta show you something."

"What?" she inquired.

Rick walked her to the van, then opened the door. He gestured for her to look inside. She stuck her head in, only to come face-to-face with Katie. Startled, Lacey shrieked. That scared Katie, so she screeched. That scared Lacey, so she shrieked again.

"Shh!" hissed Rick, pulling Lacey away from the van.

"What are you doing with that gorilla?" she demanded. "How did you get her out of the flea market?"

"I stole her," Rick explained. "And now I don't know what to do with her. Can you help me?"

"Help you?" Lacey echoed, astonished. "How?"

"Well . . . maybe you could hide her in your parents' garage," he suggested cautiously.

"What are you, bent?" she exploded. "Why don't we just hide her in my parents' bedroom?"

"Well, have you got a better idea?" he asked, frustrated.

"Yes. Leave!" she barked as she headed back to her house in a huff. "My father was right—you are weird!"

"Lacey, stop!" Rick ordered.

The sharpness of Rick's outburst made her stop. She looked back to see what else Rick had to say.

"I thought you were little Miss Animal Rights!" he said, glaring at her. "Do you really believe all that stuff, or were you just trying to get votes?"

Lacey was offended. "Of course I believe it!"

"Then prove it," Rick dared.

"B-but this is different," she stammered.

"No, it isn't!" he insisted. "This is the same thing! Katie is an innocent, defenseless animal and we have to protect her! If we don't, who will?"

Lacey's face looked as if she knew Rick had a point. She glanced past Rick toward the van. Katie was hanging out the side window, signing something.

"What is she saying?" asked Lacey.

"Pretty girl," answered Rick.

Lacey smiled. "Smart gorilla."

"Can you help her?" Rick pleaded.

Lacey sighed. "You're right. Animals can't help themselves, so someone has to do it for them. And it might as well be me. But you can't hide that gorilla around here," she stated flatly. "Sooner or later someone's going to find her."

"Then where should I take her?" asked Rick.

Lacey thought a moment, then asked, "How well do you drive?"

Rick smiled. "Just ask any cop in town."

Lacey shook her head, then said, "You're going to have to drive her to Canada. She'll be safe there."

Rick gave her a puzzled look. "Why would a gorilla be safe in Canada?"

"The cops can't touch her there. It's illegal for them to cross the border," Lacey replied. "And they can't send her back, either."

"Are you sure about this?" Rick asked doubtfully.

"It worked for my uncle Max," she answered.

Rick gave her another puzzled look. "Is your uncle Max a gorilla?"

"No," Lacey explained, "he's a hippie. And he didn't want to go to Vietnam, so he stayed in Canada during the war. The cops couldn't touch him there."

"Where is he now?" Rick asked curiously.

"In Washington State, just south of the Canadian border," she told him. "If you can get Katie up there, I bet Uncle Max'll help you sneak her over the border."

"And then she'll be safe!" exclaimed Rick. But then his face fell. "Wait a minute. I don't know how to get to

Washington. And I can't even afford to buy a map. All I have is seven dollars."

Just then the front door opened and Mr. Carr reappeared. He was holding out his watch again.

"Daddy, just two more minutes. Please," Lacey pleaded.

"The social hour is over," he said firmly.

"But Rick needs my—" she began.

"Inside, now!" he ordered.

Rick and Lacey exchanged looks.

"It's okay," Rick whispered to her. "Thanks for your help."

Lacey took a last look at Rick, then marched back into her house.

Rick couldn't help but notice Mr. Carr, who was lingering on the porch, staring at him. Rick quickly plastered a frozen smile on his face again. "Have a nice evening, Mr. Carr," he said through gritted teeth.

Mr. Carr eyed Rick suspiciously. "I don't like you, son," he said simply. "Stay away from my daughter."

Before Rick could say anything, Mr. Carr slammed the door in his face.

Rick ran back to the van, trying to remember what Lacey had told him.

"Uncle Max . . . lives in Washington . . . Canada . . ." he reminded himself.

A beam of light suddenly swept across the yard. Rick squinted up and saw Lacey at her bedroom window, aiming a flashlight at him.

She waved him over. He silently tiptoed across the lawn and stood under her window.

"Here's some stuff for your trip," she whispered, then heaved two bedrolls out the window.

They bounced off Rick's head and landed on the lawn. As Rick bent over to pick them up, a box of pretzels bopped him in the head. A second later he was hit by a falling bag of candy.

"Ouch!" he muttered, rubbing his head. He looked up just in time to see several sweaters landing on his face. They were followed by a map with her uncle's address scrawled across the top.

"Is that all?" he asked, covering his head with his hands for protection.

"No," she whispered. Then she dropped a thick wad of money held together by a rubber band. It bounced off Rick's forehead.

"Thanks, Lacey," said Rick in a hushed voice.

She smiled down at him. "Good luck!"

Margaret was lying in bed, unable to sleep. It had been a long, hard day for her—confronting Gus Charnley, losing Katie, and then having a fight with Rick.

She pulled the covers up to her chin and tried to get comfortable, but it was no good. She was too upset to sleep.

She reached for the remote control and clicked on the TV set. Maybe something on the tube would make her forget her troubles.

The TV set came alive with a news bulletin. A newsman was reporting live from outside Charnley's Flea Market.

"The search is on for a young boy and the gorilla that he kidnapped tonight," said the newsman.

Margaret sat bolt upright in bed, staring at the TV in disbelief. "No . . . it can't be," she muttered, shaking her head at the TV.

"The young fugitive made a daring escape with the priceless animal," the newsman continued.

As the news sank in, Margaret's face darkened. "Oh, no." She sighed heavily. "Rick, what have you done?"

EIGHT

RICK GOT ON THE FREEWAY, HEADING NORTH.
He was careful not to speed or do anything that would attract any attention to himself.

Katie was ecstatic. Unable to control herself, she was jumping up and down in the back of the van, hooting and barking at the top of her lungs.

"Katie out! Katie out!" she signed with excitement.

"I told you I'd get you out, didn't I?" said Rick with a laugh. "We sure showed them."

Katie suddenly loped to the front and jumped into Rick's lap, licking his face from top to bottom.

"Hey!" Rick squawked. "I can't see!"

The van swerved across three lanes of the freeway as Rick leaned around Katie's huge body, struggling to see out the windshield.

He managed to steer the van back into his lane, and then he shoved Katie off his lap.

"Katie play!" she signed. "Katie play!"

"Yeah, good," agreed Rick. "That'll occupy you for a while. What do you want to play?"

In answer, Katie jumped in Rick's lap again, only this

time she was facing front. She snatched the wheel from Rick and started steering.

"Hey—no, you can't drive!" Rick yelled.

The van lurched wildly to the right, skidding across the freeway again as Rick fought Katie for control of the wheel.

"This is not a good game, Katie! Now give me the wheel back!" he ordered.

Katie hopped out of the driver's seat and climbed up into the passenger seat.

"Good Katie," Rick signed as he settled back into his seat. He then reached into the burlap bag and pulled out Katie's Viewmaster. "You sit over there and play with your Viewmaster, okay?"

Katie's eyes lit up when she saw her favorite toy. She grabbed it from Rick and held it up, but soon she threw it down again. "No work," she signed to Rick.

"Oh, yeah," Rick said, realizing what the problem was. "You can't see anything through the eyepiece. That's because it's dark outside. There's no light. Sorry."

Katie grunted, agitated. She was obviously bored and restless.

"Man," said Rick, "you're like a little kid on a long car trip."

"Katie play!" she signed.

"Yeah, you play while I drive," Rick signed back.

Katie looked around for something to play with. The lights on the dashboard caught her attention and she started fiddling with them. She found the knob for the windshield wipers and turned them on.

Swish, swish! Swish, swish! Swish, swish!

Katie watched them work, captivated by the swinging motion they made. Her head jerked from side to side as she followed the movement of the wipers.

Then Katie discovered the radio. She cranked the volume all the way up and started flipping through the dial.

"It's ten minutes to midnight here at radio station WWBT, which is where your radio dial should always be!"

Katie was fascinated by the radio DJ's voice, and tried to figure out where it was coming from. She pawed at the speakers while Rick held his ears in pain.

Then Katie stumbled on the horn.

Beeeep! Beeeep! Beeeep!

This seemed to be her favorite game. It drove Rick crazy, but he figured anything was better than having her jump in his lap and try to drive again.

After a few hours of Katie running the wipers, blaring the radio, and blowing the horn, Rick was about to lose his mind. He finally decided to pull over for the night so they could get some sleep. After getting off the freeway, he was able to locate a deserted scenic overlook and parked there for the night.

Rick laid out the bedrolls in the back of the van and signed for Katie to get in one of them.

"Okay, it's time to sleep," Rick told Katie. "Playtime is over. You have to lie down and go to sleep."

"Katie play!" she insisted.

"Katie sleep!" he insisted.

Letting out a disappointed hoot, Katie finally relented and climbed inside her bedroll. Rick crawled into the other one and laid his weary head on his jacket, using it as a pillow.

Rick was tired from the long, stressful day, so he really wanted to sleep for a while. Katie, however, was a bundle of energy. Just as Rick drifted off to sleep she suddenly sprang out of her bedroll, landing squarely on Rick's chest.

"Oof!" he cried, wheezing for air. "Get off me, you big, hairy ape!"

Katie started wrestling with him. Rick had no choice but to wrestle back. He attacked, trying to pin Katie to the floor, but she was much too strong. She effortlessly flipped Rick off her and rolled on top of him.

"Okay, now you're gonna get it!" he warned her as he put her in a headlock.

Katie easily slipped out of it and pinned Rick to the floor.

"No fair!" he said, spitting out a mouthful of hair. "I call a time-out!"

Katie had won and she knew it. She danced around the back of the van, hooting and beating her chest.

"Okay," gasped Rick, exhausted. "It's sleep time."

Katie crawled back into her bedroll and snuggled up close to Rick. Then she opened her mouth and yawned right in Rick's face.

"Yeeeesh," he said, turning his head away from her. "This is going to be a long trip."

After getting a late start the next morning, Rick pulled off the freeway at noon to get food. Katie had scarfed all the candy and pretzels during the night and now they were both starving.

Rick parked the van in front of a small country store.

"Stay here," he signed to Katie, climbing out of the van. "Don't let anybody see you."

Katie signed something back at Rick.

"I don't think they have cheese pizza here." Rick rolled his eyes, then ran into the store.

Rick grabbed some potato chips, cupcakes, candy bars, and a couple of sodas. He plopped them on the counter, then dug in his pocket for the roll of cash Lacey had given him.

Just then a police car eased into the parking lot and stopped right next to the van. Rick's face turned ghostly white.

"We're about to be nailed," he breathed.

A burly cop stepped out of the police car and stretched his legs. Barely three feet away, Katie was bouncing in the driver's seat of the van, pretending to drive. All the cop had to do was turn his head a little to the left, and he'd be staring right at Katie!

"What was the last thing I said to her?" Rick mulled to himself, shaking his head. "I could have sworn I told her to stay out of sight."

Rick held his breath, his eyes glued to the parking lot.

The cop walked past Katie without noticing her, then sauntered into the country store. Rick quickly grabbed a nearby newspaper and buried his face in it.

The cop grabbed a package of doughnuts and got in line right behind Rick. *Stay cool,* Rick thought to himself. *Stay cool.* He flipped open the paper, pretending to be reading it—and suddenly found himself staring at a picture of Katie.

The headline under her picture read *Youth Sought in Gorilla Theft—$10,000 Reward Offered.*

Rick slapped the paper closed. His heart was beating a mile a minute.

"You want the paper too, kid?" the clerk asked.

"Yes, please," Rick said weakly, struggling to breathe. He threw some money on the counter and grabbed the bag.

He started for the door, then noticed that the van was rolling backward across the parking lot! Katie must have hit the shift knob and knocked the van out of gear.

The van bounced over the curb and started rolling down the street. It was picking up speed.

Rick broke into a run, bursting out the door and sprinting across the parking lot.

"Katie! Come back!" he yelled, chasing the van down the road.

Meanwhile, the cop looked around to see what all the yelling was about. He spotted Rick chasing after the runaway van and quickly took off after them.

Katie was hooting merrily as the van glided down the road. Rick ran after her as fast as he could, signing, "Stop! Stop!" But Katie didn't see him; she was having too much fun.

The van veered to the left, then glided off the road and down a small hill, where it rolled into a huge tree.

Whack!

The fender dug into the tree.

Rick stumbled down the hill to the van. He was relieved to see there was no damage except for a small dent in the fender.

"Katie, are you okay?" he called. But there was no answer. Rick reached for the door, but just then he heard a voice behind him.

"Is that your van, son?"

Rick looked over his shoulder and saw the cop huffing and puffing as he ran down the hill.

Rick did his best to act casual. "Uh, no, sir," he improvised, thinking as fast as he could. "It's my big brother's van."

"Where is he?" the cop demanded.

"He's . . . uh, still back at the store. I'm too young to drive, you know," Rick stated innocently.

The cop looked the van over. He was definitely suspicious.

"What's in the back?" asked the cop.

"Nothing." Rick shrugged. "Just a whole lot of nothing. Lots and lots of nothing."

"Then you won't mind if I have a look for myself, will you?" the cop asked, his hand already reaching for the door handle.

Rick started to say something, then realized he had no idea what he could possibly say, so he said nothing. His mouth simply hung open.

The cop opened the door and peered inside the van. Rick closed his eyes, prepared for the worst.

"Yep, it's empty all right."

Rick opened his eyes, shocked. "Huh? It is?"

He leaned in the door next to the cop, anxious to have a look inside. All he saw in the van were two bed-rolls and some maps. No gorilla.

"Whew, it smells like a zoo in here," the cop said, sniffing inside the van.

"Yeah, that's because my brother's a musician," Rick offered.

"Oh, I see," replied the cop, apparently trying to make sense of Rick's explanation. "Well, you wait here, son. I'm going back to the store to have a little talk with this brother of yours."

"Yes, sir," Rick said obligingly. "I'll be right here."

The cop scaled the hill and in a moment he was out of sight.

"Katie!" Rick yelled, frantically searching the area. "Where the heck are you?"

Katie stuck her head out of some nearby bushes.

"Let's go! Get over here!" Rick hollered as he jumped in the van and cranked the engine.

But Katie didn't budge. She stayed frozen in the bushes, scared.

"Come on," Rick signed to her. "We have to get out of here before that cop comes back!"

Katie still wouldn't budge. She signed, "Katie afraid Rick mad."

"Of course I'm mad!" he signed angrily. "You almost got us arrested!"

"Rick promise not to yell at Katie," she signed timidly.

Rick took a deep breath, then signed calmly, "I promise."

Relieved, Katie jumped in the van and together they drove off, heading north again.

Margaret's front yard was overrun with reporters, photographers, and TV cameramen.

When the police learned it was her son who had stolen the gorilla, it wasn't long before the press found out. And since no one knew where Rick was, the press wanted to interview the next-best person: his mother.

Every time Margaret went in or out of her house, she was surrounded by persistent reporters. They stuck lights and cameras and microphones in her face, barraging her with questions.

"Why did your son do it, Mrs. Heller?"

"What does your son plan to do with the gorilla?"

"Does your son have a criminal record?"

At first Margaret wanted nothing to do with the reporters, and tried her best to ignore them. But then she realized the reporters might be the best way to expose the cruel way Gus Charnley treated his animals.

"Ladies and gentlemen of the press," she said when all the lights and cameras and microphones were once again aimed at her. "You want to know why my son stole that gorilla? Well, it's because of a man named Gus Charnley!"

"The owner of the Charnley Flea Market?" a reporter asked.

"Yes," answered Margaret. "And although he is the legal owner of the gorilla, he doesn't deserve to have her. Mr. Charnley mistreated Katie, the same way he mistreated his other gorilla, Bobo."

"Do you have any proof of your accusations, Mrs. Heller?" another reporter wanted to know.

"No, I don't," she had to admit. "But that's why my son abducted her. He wanted to help her. He wanted to save her from Mr. Charnley and his horrible flea market."

All of the local news stations ran the story that night. And the very next morning, the reporters, photographers, and TV cameramen all converged at Gus Charnley's home. They surrounded him, barking questions, when he came outside.

"How do you answer Mrs. Heller's accusations about your being cruel to animals, Mr. Charnley?"

"Is it true you abused that poor gorilla?"

"How many other animals have you abused?"

Gus had only one thing to say: "No comment." He then jumped in his truck and raced to Margaret's house. He had plenty to say to her.

"Lady, you're ruining my reputation!" he roared when Margaret opened the door.

"Nobody could ruin *your* reputation, believe me," she stated flatly. That made Gus even angrier, if that was at all possible.

"When the cops catch that punk kid of yours, I'm pressing charges!" he promised. "They're gonna lock him up for a long time!"

"Like the way you lock up your animals?" she shot back.

Gus stared at her with an evil grin. "You're no better than me, lady. We're both putting that gorilla on display.

I do it for kids, and you do it for egghead scientists!"

"You're wrong!" declared Margaret. "I'm *teaching* her—"

He interrupted her with a laugh. "You think she wants to learn all that crap? No way! She'd rather be free, running around a damn jungle somewhere!"

Margaret was stunned into silence. Gus had made a good point.

"The bottom line is," Gus continued, "you're using her to get ahead—just like I am!"

Having spoken his mind, Gus stalked back to his truck and sped away.

Margaret was left with a lot to think about.

NINE

DETECTIVES LOU GREENBERG AND BO MARKLE were assigned to the case of the kidnapped gorilla. When the file was dropped on their desk, they were just finishing up a grand-theft-auto case.

So, after spending most of the morning sifting through paperwork, Greenberg and Markle trudged out of the precinct, got into their unmarked car, and headed over to Charnley's Flea Market to interview Gus.

They did have to make one quick stop first, though— at a drive-through Chinese restaurant, so Greenberg could satisfy his craving for dumplings. *Then* they headed over to the flea market.

"There's one thing I don't get, Bo," Greenberg was saying as he picked through his container of food.

"Are you sure you aren't underestimating yourself?" Markle quipped from behind the steering wheel. "Only one thing? That doesn't seem likely."

Greenberg pressed on, ignoring Markle's remark. "Why do they call it a flea market? I mean, it's not like you can buy fleas there. They sell tube socks and stuff. Shouldn't they call it a tube sock market?"

"Would you go shopping at a place called the Tube

Sock Market?" asked Markle. "Doesn't sound like a lot of fun."

"Yes," agreed Greenberg, stuffing a forkful of food into his mouth, "but *flea market* isn't any more inviting. So why do they call it a flea market?"

Markle shook his head. "I dunno. It ain't exactly one of those questions I lose sleep over."

Greenberg ripped open a package of soy sauce with his teeth, then squeezed the package, dripping it into his container of food. Just then Markle drove over a pothole, jostling Greenberg and causing him to squirt soy sauce all over Markle's shirt.

"Oops," said Greenberg. He picked up a napkin and started wiping his partner's shirt.

"Oops?" echoed Markle sarcastically, grabbing the napkin to wipe it himself. "That's all you can say when you ruin someone's designer shirt? Oops?"

"If that's a designer shirt, I'm Georgio Armani," said Greenberg, attacking his food again.

Markle got as much soy sauce off his shirt as possible, then tossed the napkin into the backseat.

"Remind me never to spend more than ten minutes in a car with you again," Markle stated.

Between mouthfuls, Greenberg said, "So I squeezed the soy sauce a little too hard. Shoot me."

"I'm thinking about it," Markle replied. "This car's gonna smell like dumplings for the next ten years."

"You wanna talk smell?" asked Greenberg, wiping his chin with his sleeve. "There's this new thing called mouthwash. Maybe you should try it sometime."

They reached Charnley's Flea Market and headed inside. Markle made sure to button his suit jacket to cover the huge stain on his shirt.

Inside the flea market, the *This Way to Katie* sign was missing from the wall. In its place was a new sign that read *Katie Is on Vacation—She'll Be Back Soon!*

Greenberg pointed out the sign to his partner as they made their way through the crowd to Gus's office. "Hey," remarked Greenberg, "I guess he's got a lot of faith that we're gonna find his gorilla, huh?"

"That's only because he doesn't know us very well," Markle said to him.

As they passed a large display of tube socks, Greenberg snatched up a pair to show his partner.

"See?" he said, waving them in Markle's face. "Tube socks! But do you see any fleas here?"

Markle grabbed the socks and tossed them back on the display rack, then pulled Greenberg down the aisle.

They found Gus's office and knocked.

"Get in here!" Gus ordered from the other side of the door.

"He sounds like a nice fellow," Greenberg noted to his partner before opening the door.

They went in and found Gus lighting up a big fat cigar.

"I'm Detective Greenberg and this is my partner, Detective Markle."

It was clear Gus couldn't have cared less what their names were. "It's about time!" he growled in their direction. "What'd you guys do, solve every crime in California before comin' down here?"

After abandoning the car he "borrowed" from his mom, Rick races toward the chain-link fence he knows the cops won't be able to scale.

Rick is having second thoughts about military school when he sees the alternative—cleaning up after a gorilla.

For some reason Katie is a lot more cooperative with Rick than she is with his mom, and when the gorilla offers to share her food, how can he refuse?

When Rick gives Katie a painting lesson that gets playful, his mother is furious. "I'm the teacher here," she says. "You're the janitor."

"Out. Home. Katie go home," Katie signs frantically to Rick when her owner, Gus Charnley, takes her from the research lab and puts her on display at his flea market.

Taking matters into her own hands, Katie rips the gate from her prison, and she and Rick escape into the night.

"Lady, you are ruining my reputation," Gus Charnley tells Rick's mom when she accuses Gus of mistreating his gorillas.

At a pit stop on their flight to Canada, Katie trips the emergency brake and rolls the van down a steep hill—right in front of a policeman!

Hungry, tired, and with a price on their heads, Rick and Katie wrestle on the beach for the last food they have. Rick is furious when Katie wins, and tells her, "I'm better off alone!"

But when Katie nearly drowns and Rick risks his life to save her, he realizes being alone may not be so great after all.

As they near Lacey's Uncle Max's house, Rick and Katie stop to pick a few apples from a roadside orchard. The farmer appears with a shotgun, threatening to turn them in for the reward money.

Safe from the farmer's shotgun, Rick and Katie float down the river on his fifteenth birthday.

"Katie feel bad," Katie signs to Rick as soon as they reach Uncle Max's house. Worried, Rick promises never to leave Katie again.

Caught just short of the Canadian border, Rick wonders anxiously if Katie made it safely across.

When Rick takes his case to court, Katie makes a surprise appearance and takes the stand, asking to stay with Rick instead of going back to the flea market.

Rick promised Katie he'd never leave her, but when he and his mom take Katie to Hawaii for a conference, Rick has to decide what's best for Katie—a life in captivity with her friend, or life in the jungle, where she belongs?

"No," deadpanned Greenberg, "not every crime. Only the ones that start with the letter *T*. Trespassing, tailgating . . ."

"Funny," said Gus with a frown, "real funny. I just hope you're a better cop than you are a comedian. Now, are you gonna get my gorilla back, or what?"

Markle pulled out his pad and pen. "Can you describe the gorilla for us?"

Gus shot back, "What's to describe? It's a gorilla! It's dark and hairy and it smells bad."

"That's funny—so is my mother-in-law," remarked Greenberg.

Markle continued, "What I mean is, does the gorilla have any distinguishing marks? Or clothes, maybe?"

"Clothes?" Gus said, rapidly running out of patience. "What gorilla do you know that wears clothes?"

Markle answered, "Well, you know how sometimes the dancing bear at the circus wears that funny hat. . . ."

Greenberg added, "Yeah, and sometimes the chimps wear suspenders with those little shorts."

Gus exploded, "It's not wearing any damn clothes! Now get out there and find my gorilla before they turn it into glue!"

Greenberg and Markle exchanged quick looks, then left the office.

"I think he's mistaken," Markle said as they wove their way back out of the flea market. "*Horses* are turned into glue, not gorillas."

"How do they get glue from a horse, anyway?" wondered Greenberg.

"I'm pretty sure it's in the hooves," replied Markle.

Greenberg thought about it a minute, then said, "Horses' hooves are filled with glue? Then how do they run so fast?"

Markle shook his head. "I dunno. It's for bigger minds than ours to figure out."

After driving a few hours, Rick pulled off the freeway again. Katie had eaten the snacks he'd bought at the country store, so Rick's stomach was still rumbling for food.

He maneuvered the van off the freeway and picked up a veggie burger at a drive-through place, then headed down to a deserted beach, where he and Katie wouldn't be spotted.

Once they were parked, Rick reached into the bag for his veggie burger, but Katie had already beat him to it. She had it in her hairy paws and was ready to eat it herself.

"Katie hungry," she signed, licking her lips.

"How can you be hungry?" Rick asked, aghast. "You already ate all the cupcakes, potato chips, and candy bars! Plus the candy and pretzels Lacey gave us!"

"Katie hungry," she signed, still holding the veggie burger tightly in her furry fists.

"Give me the burger!" he ordered, seeing that she was about to add it to the list of things she had already consumed. "Hand it over!"

Katie put her hands behind her back.

"Hand it over," said Rick, holding out his palm. "It's mine!"

Katie shook her head.

"Okay, we'll split it," he offered, trying to grab the burger away from her.

Katie held it out of his reach. Rick made another frantic grab for it, but by then Katie had already dived out the van window. She charged across the sand, proudly waving the burger over her head.

Rick was in hot pursuit. He tackled Katie as she frantically unwrapped the wax paper. Rick tried desperately to pry it away from her, but she was much stronger.

"You're skating on thin ice, Katie!" he bellowed.

Katie stuffed the entire burger into her mouth, swallowing it whole. Then she burped happily.

Rick jumped to his feet, suddenly angry. "I can't believe I have to wrestle a gorilla for my dinner! I've had it with you!"

Katie licked her lips. She had no idea why Rick was mad.

"Just leave me alone!" he demanded. "I'm tired of being responsible for you!"

Katie cocked her head, studying Rick curiously.

"Don't you get it?" he signed angrily. "I'm better off alone."

It was obvious Katie knew what the word *alone* meant. With a hurt look on her face, she wandered over to a nearby hill and started climbing to the top, giving Rick some time to be alone. At the top of the hill, which was about thirty feet high, stood a large tree, its branches swaying with the ocean breeze. When Katie reached the tree she started swinging on the lowest branch, hooting dejectedly.

"Katie, get off there!" Rick called from down on the beach. "It's not safe."

But before Katie could do anything . . .

Crack!

The branch suddenly snapped in half and Katie fell over the edge of the hill, splashing into the water below.

"No!" Rick cried helplessly as he raced into the surf. He knew gorillas couldn't swim, so if he didn't save her quickly, she would drown.

Rick dove into the cold, swirling water and swam to Katie, who was freaking out. She had never been in water before and had no idea what it was. All she knew was she didn't like it. Rick grabbed her by the scruff of her neck and started swimming back to shore.

"Hang on!" he hollered, panting wildly. "You're gonna be okay!"

Rick struggled to paddle them to shore, finally reaching the point where he could stand up. Gulping in deep breaths of air, he dragged Katie out of the surf and onto the beach. They were both covered from head to foot in seaweed.

Rick sat on the beach, hugging Katie. Having almost lost her just then made him realize being alone wasn't so great after all.

Rick and Katie sat on the beach, watching the sun sink into the ocean. They had a small fire going, which offered some warmth against the cool night air. Katie was huddled inside her bedroll, shivering. Rick was sitting next to her, drawing a picture.

Having found some paper and a Magic Marker in the van, he was drawing a picture of himself and Katie. In the picture, they were standing on the beach together, watching the sun go down.

Katie watched his hand making elegant strokes on the paper. "Good," she signed, clearly impressed.

"Thanks." Rick smiled. "It's the only thing I'm good at. My dad always liked my drawings, too."

Katie gave him a puzzled look. "What is *dad?*" she signed.

"A dad is someone who shows you how to ride a bike and throw a ball. And then he disappears and never comes back," he signed bitterly.

Katie clearly didn't understand. She slapped her forehead.

"Come on, go to bed," Rick signed, anxious to end the discussion. He could feel tears welling up in his eyes. He didn't want Katie to see him crying, so he turned away from her.

Katie hooted to get his attention. Then she signed, "Eyes wet! Eyes wet!"

"My eyes are not wet!" he blurted out, annoyed because she had caught him crying. "Now go to sleep!"

Katie crawled deeper inside her bedroll and before long she was snoring loudly.

A few minutes later Rick slipped out of his bedroll, being careful not to wake Katie. He knew his mom must be worried about him, so he figured he'd better call home and let her know he and Katie were all right. He was also getting pretty homesick, but he wasn't going to tell her that part.

Rick walked to a public phone near the road and dialed his number. It rang and rang.

"She's probably driving around looking for me," he said under his breath.

The answering machine clicked on and Margaret's voice came through the receiver. Hearing it made him even more homesick.

"Hi, this is Margaret. Leave a message after the beep."

Rick swallowed his tears and left her a message.

TEN

MARGARET CAME HOME AND COLLAPSED, TO-
tally exhausted. She had been driving around all night
long, searching for her son and the stolen gorilla.

She noticed the red light flashing on the answering
machine and hit the play button, praying it was a message from Rick.

"Hi, Mom. It's me, Rick," came the voice from the machine.

"Thank God!" said Margaret, relieved. She knelt close
to the machine, listening to Rick's message.

"I just wanted to let you know I'm okay. I guess I'm in
a lot of trouble, and you're real mad at me. . . ." Rick's
voice trailed off. His voice sounded brave, but Margaret
could tell it was an act. She could hear the fear behind
his words.

"I just wanted to say I'm sorry for the way I've been
acting since Dad left. See . . . I'm learning how hard it is
to take care of somebody all by yourself. It's tough. . . ."

Margaret realized her little boy was starting to grow
up. It made her feel happy *and* sad at the same time.

"Anyway," the message continued, "everything's
gonna be all right. I promise. Bye."

When the message ended Margaret broke into tears. "Happy birthday, Rick," she whispered.

After driving another six hours, Rick finally reached Lacey's uncle's house, which he found sitting alone in a stretch of desolate farmland, just a few miles south of the Canadian border.

Rick stopped the van near an old, beat-up mailbox that sat at the end of a fog-shrouded driveway.

"This is the address," Rick said, peering out the window. Squinting through the fog, he could barely make out the shape of a house at the other end of the walkway.

"You better wait here," signed Rick, climbing out of the van.

He walked a few steps farther and then noticed what appeared to be a large group of people standing in the front yard.

"Hello," he called out, but nobody answered.

He walked a few more steps, and through the fog he could see another cluster of people standing on the lawn.

"Hello there," he called out again, but nobody answered this time either. They didn't even move.

"What's the matter? Are you people deaf?" he yelled.

There was no movement. Rick was starting to get spooked. Mustering his courage, he started moving toward the crowd of people.

That's when he noticed they weren't people at all. They were statues. The yard was littered with dozens of different kinds of marble statues—Roman soldiers, religious figures, and even sports heroes.

"I guess I don't look too stupid," Rick mumbled to himself, "standing here in the middle of nowhere talking to statues. . . ."

"Don't take another step!" a bellowing voice said from somewhere in the fog.

Rick nearly jumped out of his shoes. He looked around. The voice seemed to come from one of the statues.

"Mr. Carr? Max Carr?" Rick called out.

"Who wants to know?" came the question from somewhere among the many statues.

"I'm Rick Heller, your niece's classmate," said Rick. "She sent me here. She said you could help me sneak my friend into Canada."

Uncle Max stepped out from behind a statue, revealing himself. He was a tall man with scraggly hair and a messy beard.

"Yeah, she called me," muttered Uncle Max. "Where's your friend?"

Rick turned back and yelled into the fog. "Katie! Come here!"

Uncle Max looked over just as the gorilla appeared out of the fog. His jaw nearly hit the ground.

"Just what the heck is that?" he sputtered.

"It's a gorilla," Rick explained.

"I know that!" Uncle Max shot back. "What the heck is it doing in my front yard?"

"It's not an 'it,'" Rick corrected. "Her name is Katie, and she's the friend you're supposed to be helping me sneak into Canada."

"Lacey never said your friend was an ape!" he yelled. "Are you nuts, kid?"

"No, sir," replied Rick. "I'm just desperate. Can you help us?"

"No," he replied flatly. "In the first place, I don't want any trouble. And in the second place, it can't be done, anyway."

"Why not?" asked Rick, refusing to give up.

"Because you can't just mosey over the Canadian border with a gorilla. They arrest people for stuff like that. And I can't afford to get arrested right now—I'm too busy with my statue business," explained Uncle Max. "I sell these to collectors in Canada. So you two better just be on your way."

Katie suddenly moaned, leaning against Rick for support. She didn't look well at all.

"What's the matter?" Rick asked.

She signed to Rick, "Katie feel bad." Rick felt her forehead. It was burning up.

"Jeez, you're sick, girl," Rick said, getting worried.

"Oh, great." Uncle Max threw up his arms. "Okay, bring her inside, but if she pukes on anything, she's history!"

Lacey had been following the news closely ever since Katie's kidnapping. She had a small TV in her bedroom, which she kept tuned to the news channel, listening for any updates on the story. She hadn't heard anything new all day, so she hoped that meant Rick hadn't been caught.

Lacey considered calling her uncle Max again to see if Rick and Katie had arrived yet, but thought she'd better wait until her parents were asleep before getting on the phone to him.

"Telephone for you, Lacey."

Mr. Carr was standing in her bedroom doorway, dressed in his bathrobe and pajamas. "Why in the world is Uncle Max calling you?" he asked, somewhat puzzled.

Lacey jumped out of bed. "Gee, he probably just wants to see if there's anything special I want for my birthday," she said, throwing on her slippers and heading down the staircase three steps at a time.

"But your birthday isn't for another five months," Mr. Carr said, tagging along behind her.

"Oh, you know how Uncle Max is," Lacey offered as an explanation. She hit the bottom of the stairs and took a sharp turn into the living room.

"Yeah," mused Mr. Carr. "He's three bricks shy of a load. Anyway, he sure seems upset about something."

"He does?" Lacey hesitated, then picked up the receiver.

Mr. Carr wandered into the kitchen. Lacey waited until he was out of sight, then put the phone to her ear.

"Hello, Uncle Max," she chirped.

"A gorilla!" he yelled back. "A gorilla, for goodness sake! And not just any gorilla—a *hot* gorilla! Why did you do this to me? We're family, for crying out loud! Is this how you treat family? You dump a hot gorilla in their lap?"

Yep, Lacey concluded, *Uncle Max is upset, all right.* There was no mistake about that. Lacey listened to his tirade, waiting for a chance to get a word in.

"I told Rick you'd help him!" she whispered into the phone as soon as Uncle Max paused to take a breath.

"Forget it!" he yelled back. Lacey imagined his face was starting to turn a deep shade of red. "Look, Lacey, I got a nice life here collecting junk! I don't need *Wild Kingdom* in my living room! Let this kid save the apes somewhere else!"

"You used to tell me always to do the right thing!" Lacey said scornfully, her voice rising. "That's all Rick is trying to do—the right thing! And he needs your help!"

There was a pause while Uncle Max considered this for a moment. Lacey held her breath. Her uncle had indeed said all that to her, but it had been a long time ago. Uncle Max was a lot older now.

"Yeah, well . . ." Uncle Max hemmed and hawed. "I've changed since then. I'm tired now. Too tired to get involved in this mess. So you tell your friend and his sick gorilla to take a long walk off a short tree."

"Sick?" Lacey echoed, suddenly alarmed. "Katie's sick? What's wrong with her?"

"What do you think I am, a monkey doctor?" Uncle Max said, his voice dripping with angry sarcasm.

"Lacey, get in here on the double!" Mr. Carr was bellowing from the kitchen. Something was definitely wrong.

"Uncle Max, don't do anything until I talk to you again!" Lacey ordered into the phone, then quickly hung up before he could say anything.

"What is it, Dad?" she called out innocently as she made her way down the hallway. The minute she poked her head in the kitchen and saw her father staring at the TV set, her stomach started knotting up.

"Isn't that the weird kid from the other night?"

Mr. Carr was pointing at the TV screen. The surveillance-camera tape that showed Rick chasing Katie through the flea market was being played on the news.

"Well," Lacey stammered, "i-it kind of looks like him. But you know how boys all look alike."

Mr. Carr fixed his daughter with a suspicious stare. "According to the news, he kidnapped a gorilla around ten o'clock the other night, which would have been about half an hour before he came knocking on our door," he said, tapping his trusty watch again. "Lacey, are you mixed up in this?"

Lacey crumbled. She knew she couldn't tell a bald-faced lie to her father.

"I . . . I just gave him some money, that's all." The words came out in a whisper.

Mr. Carr exploded. "That's *all?*" He grabbed the nearest telephone and started dialing, punching the numbers with a lot more force than necessary.

"What are you doing?" Lacey asked timidly.

"A little thing called damage control," was all he said as he put the phone to his ear. "Operator, give me the number for the police department."

"No!" shrieked Lacey, grabbing for the phone. "You can't do that! Daddy, you don't understand!"

"You're right—I don't understand!" he snapped at her. "I don't understand how my daughter could behave this way. Now go to your room!"

Lacey knew there was no talking to him when he was this angry. She also knew there was no way to convince him not to call the police. There was only one alternative left.

78

She turned on her heel and ran upstairs to her room, slamming the door behind her. Then she started packing a suitcase.

Twenty minutes later, Mr. Carr knocked on her bedroom door. When Lacey didn't answer, he opened the door and found the room empty. The window was open and it was obvious she had climbed out.

Greenberg and Markle were standing in the hallway outside Lacey's bedroom, waiting to question her.

"She's gone," an alarmed Mr. Carr said, peering out the open window at the darkened neighborhood.

Greenberg stepped into the room. "Any idea where she might have gone?"

Markle followed Greenberg into the room. "Did she have any visitors tonight? Any strange phone calls?"

Mr. Carr shook his head. "No . . ." Then he snapped his fingers. "Wait a second! Her uncle Max! He called about half an hour ago!"

Greenberg and Markle exchanged looks. *Bingo!*

"Exactly where does this Uncle Max reside?" Markle asked, pulling out his pad and pen.

"Washington State," replied Mr. Carr.

"Looks like we'll be taking a little plane trip tonight," remarked Greenberg.

Markle made a face. "Damn . . . I hate flying."

"I'm a paramedic, not a veterinarian!" expostulated Bob. He was standing over Katie, who was lying on Uncle Max's sofa and looking weak. Uncle Max hadn't known whom else to call for a sick gorilla, so he had asked his buddy Bob to come take a look at her.

"Can't you do anything for her?" asked Rick. "She's sick."

"Yeah," agreed Uncle Max. "Just make believe she's a person. A really hairy person."

Bob shrugged, then opened his medical bag. "I can try."

He sat beside Katie, who was shivering under a wool blanket. He tried putting a tongue depressor in her mouth, but Katie wanted to eat it. Then he tried putting a thermometer in her mouth, but she wanted to eat that too.

"At least she still has an appetite," said Bob. He gave up trying to stick anything in her mouth and instead felt the back of her neck.

"She's running a temp," he said.

"Even I knew that!" snapped Rick.

Bob ignored him, since he was just a kid. "We need to get her into some cool water. That'll bring her temperature down," he informed them. "Max, go fill up your tub."

"Whoa, hold on," interjected Rick. "Gorillas hate water. Especially Katie. She almost drowned yesterday. There's no way she'll get into a tub full of water."

Bob looked Rick in the eyes. "Either she gets into the water or she lies here with a high temperature until she slips into a coma. It's that simple."

"Besides," said Uncle Max, "she's too weak to fight back right now, anyhow."

Rick looked down at Katie's bloodshot eyes and knew

that Uncle Max was right. She was in no condition to put up a fight.

The three of them lifted Katie and carried her into Uncle Max's bathroom. They set Katie down in the tub, then started to run the water slowly.

Katie rested her head on the back of the tub. Rick couldn't tell if she even realized she was lying in water, she looked so out of it. He ran into the bedroom and snatched a pillow off the bed, then put it under Katie's head.

"Now what do we do?" Rick asked Bob.

"We wait."

Rick sat with Katie while she soaked, keeping her company.

"It's all my fault," he told her when they were alone. "I was supposed to be taking care of you."

Katie was too tired to respond. She grunted half-heartedly, then reached for her Viewmaster. Rick helped hold it up so she could peer into the eyepiece. Then she motioned for him to look through it.

Rick looked into the eyepiece and saw a 3-D picture of an African rain forest.

"Home," Katie signed.

"Yeah, I know," responded Rick softly. "Listen, Katie, you gotta get better. If you're thinking about dying on me, forget it!"

Katie wearily lifted her hands and signed, "Rick want alone."

"No!" Rick choked. "I was wrong! I'm not better off alone! We have to stick together! And if we make it to Canada, I promise I'll never leave you again!"

Katie looked at Rick, and he thought he could see trust in her eyes. "Promise. Friend," she signed weakly.

Rick hugged her tightly. She wrapped her arms around him, hugging back with all her strength.

After a moment Katie's eyes fluttered closed, and pretty soon she was snoring like a lumberjack.

Late that night, Katie's fever broke.

"Her lungs sound much better," reported Bob, who was listening to Katie's chest with a stethoscope. She was able to sit up again and her eyes were bright and clear.

Katie signed, "Katie eat."

Bob stared at her, bewildered.

"What the heck is she doing?" he asked.

"Sign language," answered Rick. "That's how we communicate."

Bob laughed. "Gorillas are just dumb animals. They can't understand something like sign language."

"You wanna test her?" dared Rick.

Uncle Max spoke up, anxious to get in on this. "There's a cantaloupe in my fridge. Tell her to go help herself."

Rick signed to Katie. Before he even finished she was up and running into the kitchen. Uncle Max and Bob followed her, intrigued.

Katie yanked the refrigerator door open and started pulling containers out, sniffing them. She tossed all the food on the floor, excitedly searching for the cantaloupe. She finally found it in the bottom drawer and held it over her head, hooting excitedly.

"That's pretty damn clever," Bob had to admit.

"Katie's smart," Rick said proudly.

Amused, they all watched Katie rip into the cantaloupe, stuffing huge chunks into her mouth.

Suddenly they heard a loud knocking. Someone was banging on the front door!

"Cops!" Rick cried.

"Hide the gorilla!" yelled Uncle Max.

"Hide me too!" squealed Bob.

Uncle Max opened a closet door. "In here!" he whispered frantically.

Rick, Katie, and Bob jammed themselves into the tiny closet, practically on top of each other. Uncle Max tried to shut the door, but half of Katie was still hanging out.

"Move in farther!" he ordered hoarsely.

"There is no farther in here!" Rick yelled from inside the closet. "My face is already up against the wall!"

Knock! Knock! Knock!

This time it was more insistent. Uncle Max had no choice but to slam the door, squeezing the occupants together. Then he heard them moan in unison.

"Keep quiet!" Uncle Max reminded them, then walked casually to the door and opened it.

"Good evening, officers," Uncle Max began, but the words died in his throat when he saw who was standing outside the door.

"Lacey!" he hollered. "What the heck are you doing here?"

"Trying to save Rick and Katie," she retorted. "Can I come in?"

Uncle Max shrugged, then waved her inside.

"I haven't had a visitor in six years," he said, "and now I've got half a softball team in my kitchen."

"Where?" Lacey asked.

Uncle Max reached over and opened the closet door. Rick, Katie, and Bob tumbled out onto the floor in a heap.

Rick pushed Katie off him, then looked up and saw Lacey standing over him. He looked more than a little surprised.

"Lacey! Uh, hi," he said nervously, jumping to his feet. "How did you get here?"

"By way of airplane," she quipped, "thanks to my father's credit card. I just hope he's in a good mood when he opens his next Visa statement."

"Why are you here?" Uncle Max asked pointedly.

"I figure as long as I'm involved in this, I may as well go all the way," she answered. "All the way to Canada, that is."

"No way," Rick said adamantly. "You can't go with us."

"Why not?" she wanted to know.

"Because we might get caught," he told her.

"Why don't we ask Katie if she wants me to go?" suggested Lacey.

"She has no say in this," Rick said.

"What's the matter, Rick?" she asked with a grin. "Are you afraid she'll say yes?"

Rick had no choice but to accept her challenge. He signed to Katie, "Do you want Lacey to come to Canada with us?"

Katie answered by reaching over and hugging Lacey. Rick threw up his hands, defeated.

"I think that means yes," declared Lacey.

"It doesn't matter," Uncle Max said glumly, "because we're not going to Canada. I'm not sneaking a gorilla over the border, so forget it."

He stalked off, hoping to put an end to the discussion right there. To his dismay, Lacey followed him into the living room. She was far from finished.

"Uncle Max," she said firmly, "I've always looked up to you, in spite of what Daddy says."

Uncle Max's left eye twitched. "What? What does he say?"

"Never mind that," Lacey said. "But I always thought you were a man who believed in things. You always told me never to give up when I believed in something, remember?"

Uncle Max did remember. That's why he didn't have a comeback for her. He stood silent for a minute, staring into Lacey's youthful, innocent eyes—eyes that, unlike his own, were still full of hopes and dreams for the future.

"I know I'm gonna regret this," Uncle Max said, his voice barely audible, "but what the heck."

Lacey jumped into his arms and gave him a big bear hug.

ELEVEN

JUST AFTER DAWN, FOUR POLICE CARS QUIETLY approached Uncle Max's house and stopped. Greenberg and Markle got out of the lead car and walked silently past the statues in the yard.

Meanwhile, the other cops searched Rick's van, which was still parked out front. Finding it empty, they surrounded the house.

"Hey, Bo," Greenberg whispered to Markle as they were creeping toward the door. "Can I kick the door in this time?"

"No way!" answered Markle. "You got to kick it in last time!"

"I did?" Greenberg asked, slightly puzzled. "I don't remember kicking in the door last time."

"Well, you did!" Markle whispered insistently. "So I get to kick it in this time."

They reached the front door and took their positions.

"Police! You're all under arrest!" Greenberg announced as Markle kicked in the front door.

The two men rushed inside, where they found Bob sound asleep on the couch in his underwear. The rest of the cops poured inside the house and split up, searching all of the rooms.

"Wake him up," Markle told Greenberg.

Greenberg shook his head. "You got to kick in the door, so you have to wake up the suspect. That's a rule."

Markle put his gun away, then reached down and shook Bob. "Wake up, pal. The police are here," the detective said softly.

Bob slowly stirred, opening his eyes. Then he suddenly realized what was going on. He jumped up and pulled his pants on.

"You Max Carr?" Greenberg asked.

"Heck, no!" Bob yelled, looking scared half to death. "I'm Bob, a friend of his."

The cops rushed back into the living room, empty-handed.

"The house is empty," one of them reported.

Greenberg kicked a nearby chair. "I hate when that happens."

His partner stepped over to Bob. "Where is he?" Markle demanded. "Where'd he go with that kid and the gorilla?"

Bob shrugged, trying to look innocent. "Beats me."

Greenberg sniffed the air with a sour look on his face. "It smells like a zoo in here. They couldn't have been gone too long."

Markle signaled for the cops to follow him out. "Let's get out an APB on Max Carr's vehicle—they're probably still close by."

*   *   *

Uncle Max, Rick, Lacey, and Katie were indeed nearby. They had left in Uncle Max's panel truck only moments before the cops showed up, and were now headed for the Canadian border.

Their plan was simple. Uncle Max had loaded up the back of his truck with statues from the yard. When they got to Canada, he would tell the border guards he was delivering the statues to a collector in Canada. They were hoping that when the border guards looked in the back, they wouldn't notice that one of the statues was actually Katie covered in white powder! When she stood posed among the other statues, frozen in an attack position, she looked just like a real statue.

Rick was scared they'd get caught and Katie would be taken away from him forever. And no matter what, Rick couldn't let that happen, not after the promise he had made to her.

"Relax, kid," Uncle Max advised Rick as he drove the last few miles to the border. "We'll make it. I got a good feeling." Just as Uncle Max finished saying that, he glanced in the rearview mirror and saw a police car speeding toward them. "Of course, sometimes my feelings are wrong," he muttered.

"What do we do?" asked Lacey with growing alarm.

Uncle Max gave her a quick wink. "I'll tell you what we *don't* do. We don't give up," he said, punching the gas pedal to the floor. "We never give up when we believe in something."

Uncle Max's truck lurched down the highway, picking up speed.

"Hold on, Katie! We're going for it!" yelled Rick into the back of the truck. Katie was holding on to a statue of Julius Caesar for dear life as the truck rattled and rolled under her feet. Small clouds of white powder rose off her every time she moved.

Three more cop cars had joined the chase, with their lights flashing and their sirens blaring. Up ahead, Uncle Max's truck was rapidly approaching a railroad crossing.

All of a sudden the crossing gates started to come down. Rick and Lacey looked down the track and saw that a train was coming. Katie saw it, too.

"Train! Train!" she signed frantically as she jumped in the front seat next to Rick and Lacey, covering them with white powder.

"We know," he signed back.

"Too late to stop now," announced Uncle Max as he sped toward the crossing. "We'll just have to beat it." He floored the accelerator. It was going to be close—real close.

Uncle Max's truck crashed through the gates and sped across the train tracks. Barely a second later, the train roared past the crossing. It whizzed by so close that the front of the train knocked the spare tire off the back of Uncle Max's truck—it shot straight up into the air, then fell back to earth, bouncing off the hood of the truck with a whump and then rolling away.

Uncle Max, Rick, and Lacey sat breathless, recovering from their close call. Katie, on the other hand, was in heaven.

"Again! Again!" she signed, hooting gleefully.

"No way are we doing that again!" Rick signed back. "Not in this lifetime."

Katie let out a disappointed whimper.

"We better get moving," Uncle Max said, throwing the truck in gear. "That train won't hold those police cars back there much longer!" Uncle Max pushed the accelerator pedal down again and the truck sped off in a hurry.

The police cars squealed to a stop on the other side of the tracks. The passing train blocked them from going any farther.

"We've been cut off!" yelled one of the cops into his car radio, watching the train roll by. "We lost 'em!"

"Don't worry," Greenberg's voice came back over the radio. "We're ready and waiting for them!"

Uncle Max's truck crested a small hill, then ran smack into a roadblock. Three police cars were sitting in the middle of the road. Greenberg and Markle were waiting beside their parked car, their guns ready.

Suddenly the truck veered off the road. Taken completely by surprise, Greenberg and Markle could only watch as it crashed through a barbed-wire fence and plowed into a cornfield.

"Wow," said Greenberg, "just like on TV."

"Let's go!" Markle cried. They all jumped in their cars and took off. One by one the cop cars followed Uncle Max's path into the cornfield. The cops couldn't see the truck through the thick wall of stalks, but that didn't matter. All they had to do was follow the clear path that had been dug out by the truck.

Up ahead, Uncle Max's truck was tearing through the cornfield, chewing up the six-foot-tall cornstalks like some kind of giant lawn mower.

"Anyone for creamed corn?" joked Uncle Max.

Lacey made a face. "That was really bad, Uncle Max."

"Hey, I've heard worse jokes," said Rick.

"You've *made* worse jokes, you mean," corrected Lacey.

"Well, on the serious side," Uncle Max said, "we need to come up with a plan. We can't keep running like this. Sooner or later we're gonna either run out of cornfield or run out of gas."

"You want a plan?" Rick asked, his face suddenly breaking into a wide grin. "I'll give you a plan!"

"Well, let's hear it!" demanded Lacey.

"It's simple," explained Rick. "Stop the truck."

Uncle Max and Lacey looked at Rick as though he were crazy.

"Trust me," insisted Rick.

Uncle Max shrugged. "Okay . . ." He slammed on the brakes.

As soon as the truck had stopped, Rick said, "Now everybody out."

Nobody moved.

"*Everybody out!*" Rick hollered, throwing open the door. "Now! Move! Go!"

Stunned, Uncle Max and Lacey climbed out, stepping into the cornfield.

"You too," Rick signed to Katie. "Katie out."

Katie gave Rick a fearful look. "Katie stay Rick," she signed.

"Katie will stay with Rick, I promise!" he signed back as fast as he could. "But right now you have to go with Lacey and Uncle Max! Please! I'll see you soon!"

"Promise?" she signed back.

Rick signed, "Promise."

Katie jumped out hesitantly, never taking her eyes off Rick. Then Rick slid into the driver's seat and pulled the door shut.

"Take care of Katie," Rick ordered, handing Lacey the Viewmaster. "No matter what, don't let them get her. That's all that matters."

"Be careful shifting into third," warned Uncle Max. "Sometimes it sticks."

Rick saw the frightened look on Katie's face. Wanting to reassure her, he quickly signed, "Love hug Katie."

"Love hug Rick," she signed back, hooting sadly.

Rick gunned the truck and took off through the cornfield.

"What's he doing?" Lacey asked.

"Sacrificing himself," Uncle Max answered as they watched the truck getting farther and farther away. Behind them, they could hear the cop cars approaching.

"C'mon," Uncle Max snapped, "we gotta hide."

Uncle Max and Lacey took Katie's hands and led her into the tall stalks, where they could no longer be seen.

A few seconds later the three cop cars whizzed by, following the truck's path through the field.

*   *   *

Rick sped through the cornfield. The truck emerged on the other side and slid into a ditch.

"Oh, no!" Rick exclaimed, throwing the truck into reverse and hitting the gas.

The truck spun around, kicking up a thick spray of mud. Its wheels spinning, it finally lurched out of the ditch and back onto solid ground.

Rick shifted into first gear and tore up a small hill, crashing through another fence and bouncing onto the other side of the freeway.

"Let's see you catch me now, turkeys!" Rick taunted the cops as he slid into the fast lane.

The cops must have heard him somehow, because just then four more cop cars appeared on the horizon. They were headed straight toward the truck!

Rick spun the wheel to avoid a head-on collision. The truck swerved to the right, smashing into a road sign before plunging into another ditch with a loud thunk.

The cops pulled over and jumped out of their cars, guns drawn. They raced down the hill and found the truck lying in the ditch.

"Everyone out of the vehicle!" Markle ordered as the rest of the cops surrounded the truck. "Come out with your hands up!"

The driver's-side door of the truck creaked open and the statue of Julius Caesar toppled out, landing face-down in the ditch.

Then Rick calmly stepped out, with his hands over his head.

He was immediately tackled by two cops, who wasted no time handcuffing him. Meanwhile, Greenberg checked the truck, only to find it empty of anything living.

"What the . . . ?" he muttered, then looked at his partner. "It's empty. He's pulled a David Copperfield on us!"

"I hate when that happens!" Markle ranted, kicking a tire. His voice echoed over the cornfield. Then he turned on Rick. "Where are the others? And the gorilla?"

"I ditched them," Rick said with a boyish grin. "They never came up with any gas money. They always fell asleep at the tolls, too."

"Read this punk his rights!" Markle growled.

Rick was led up the hill and placed inside the back of a cop car. Then one of the cops started reading Rick his rights.

"Listen up. You have the right to remain silent. You have the right . . ."

As the cop droned on, Rick looked out the car window. Way over on the other side of the cornfield he could see Uncle Max, Lacey, and Katie. They had doubled back through the cornfield and were slipping out the other side, making their escape along the railroad tracks.

Rick breathed a deep sigh of relief.

TWELVE

THE DAY AFTER HE HAD BEEN BROUGHT BACK to California, Rick was taken out of his cell at juvenile hall and led down a long corridor to the visitors' area. As soon as the guard ushered Rick into the drab concrete room, he saw his mother waiting for him. Rick froze. He knew he was in big trouble and was expecting his mom to be really mad.

To his surprise, she ran over and hugged him tightly. Rick hugged her back with all his strength.

"Where's Katie?" he whispered into her ear, concerned.

"She's safe," Margaret murmured quietly so the guards wouldn't hear. "A friend of Max's is hiding her on a farm in Vancouver."

Rick was relieved. "She made it over the border!"

"Thanks to you," Margaret added.

"Mom . . ." Rick said hesitantly, "I'm sorry about all this."

"Don't be," she replied firmly. "I'm proud of you."

Rick was caught off guard. "You are?" he questioned.

"You did the right thing," she said, nodding. "Maybe it wasn't legal, but it was still the right thing to do."

"What happens now?" asked Rick.

Margaret looked down. "I don't know. This is one time I wish your father were here. He'd know what to do."

Rick looked his mother straight in the eye. "But he's not here, Mom. And if he wanted to leave, then he didn't deserve us anyway," he said. "Besides, we have all the family we need."

As Margaret hugged Rick again he could see the gleam of tears in her eyes.

The next day Margaret returned to juvenile hall, this time bringing a lawyer named Dan Woodley with her. Rick couldn't help but notice how jittery the guy was. Rick thought it was as if he itched all the time or something.

Mr. Woodley came into the visitors' area and plopped his briefcase down on the table. He fumbled it open and pulled out a huge wad of papers. Then he shuffled them nervously a couple of times.

Rick was tempted to ask Mr. Woodley if he usually won his cases, but then he thought better of it. "Nice to meet you, Mr. Woodley," he said instead.

"The D.A. has offered you the following deal," Mr. Woodley said, getting right down to business. "You plead guilty to reduced charges, and they'll agree to probation instead of time in a youth facility. It means you'll walk out of here a free man."

"It sounds too good to be true," said Rick suspiciously.

Mr. Woodley continued, "Of course, you'll have to tell them where the gorilla is. . . ."

"I knew it was too good to be true!" said Rick, then gave his mother a look. "Where did you find this dork?"

"Hear him out," Margaret scolded.

"But I'm not guilty! I didn't do anything wrong!" Rick insisted.

"I know that. You know that. But the law doesn't know that," said Mr. Woodley.

"I don't care about the law." Rick glared at him. "The law sucks."

Mr. Woodley cleared his throat, then leaned closer to Rick, speaking in a hushed tone.

"Trust me on this one, Ricky," he said. "I can call you Ricky, can't I?"

"No," said Rick flatly.

Mr. Woodley began again. "Trust me on this one, Rick. In a perfect world, things might be different. But this isn't a perfect world. This is California. As your lawyer, I have to tell you a plea bargain is your only way out."

If Mr. Woodley had expected his speech to be convincing, Rick thought, he was in for a big disappointment. "I'm not pleading to anything," stated Rick without hesitation. "And I'm not about to tell them where Katie is. So forget it." He sat back and folded his arms. As far as he was concerned, this discussion was over.

Mr. Woodley looked to Margaret for help.

"Don't look at me," she said. "It's Rick's decision."

The lawyer looked back at Rick. Rick was staring at him stone-faced, in silent defiance.

"Ricky—uh, I mean Rick," Mr. Woodley said, getting even more fidgety, "you understand that you could be looking at time behind bars, right? Possibly years."

Rick nodded.

"Is this gorilla worth that to you?"

Without even thinking, Rick said, "Yes."

Mr. Woodley gave up. He reshuffled his papers one more time, then put them back in his briefcase.

"You're making this case tough, Rick," he announced, heading for the door. "You're making it real hard to win."

"Well, do you usually win your cases?" Rick couldn't resist asking.

Rick had never been in a courtroom before. He had come close a couple of times in the past, but until now his mom had always come to his rescue. This time, however, Rick was going on trial and there was nothing his mom or anyone else could do to stop it.

He was seated in the courtroom, at the defense table. Sitting next to him was Mr. Woodley, who looked especially nervous. He kept taking his papers out of his briefcase and reshuffling them, over and over again.

Rick looked around the courtroom. His mom was sitting in the first row of seats, next to Lacey. Uncle Max was in the row behind them. Over at the prosecutor's table, Gus was sitting with his lawyer, a sleazy-looking man named Ed Price.

The judge came into the courtroom, and before Rick knew it, the trial was under way.

"It's true my client stole the gorilla," began Mr. Woodley, making his opening statement to the courtroom. "But we will prove he had a moral obligation to free Katie from Gus Charnley's Plexiglas prison."

Then Gus's lawyer got up to make his opening statement.

"Your Honor, we will prove this is an open-and-shut case of breaking and entering, and grand theft," he stated, pointing at Rick, "perpetrated by a rebellious youth who has never demonstrated one bit of moral fiber in his entire life."

Rick flinched, hearing the lawyer bad-mouth him like that—especially since what he said was true.

After the opening statements, Rick's lawyer called Gus to the stand, hoping to show the judge just how cruel Gus was.

"Did you know that Katie could speak sign language?" Mr. Woodley asked Gus. "Did you know she has a vocabulary of over one thousand words?"

Gus smirked. "Then how come I never heard her complain about the way I treated her?"

The courtroom burst into laughter. Mr. Woodley shot a worried glance at Rick at the defense table as his hands started to tremble.

"Mr. Charnley," he continued, "you had another gorilla by the name of Bobo, isn't that right?"

Gus looked down at the floor, shaking his head. "Yeah," he said sadly. "I sure miss my Bobo."

"Wasn't Bobo usually withdrawn and depressed?" asked Mr. Woodley.

"What are you talkin' about?" scoffed Gus. "Depressed? Yeah, and I sent him to a shrink twice a week!"

There was more laughter. Mr. Woodley's jitters were getting worse.

"Bobo was a happy gorilla, make no mistake about it," proclaimed Gus sharply. "He loved kids and he loved the flea market! That gorilla lived happy and died happy! And I don't mind tellin' you, I shed a tear when he croaked."

Gus looked like he was about to cry right there on the witness stand. Mr. Woodley wasn't buying it, though.

"If you cared for Bobo so much, then why did you regularly leave him in his cage with no food or water?" the attorney wanted to know.

Gus's face instantly turned angry. "Hey, who said I did that?" he snapped. "I'll break their legs!"

Mr. Price leapt to his feet. "Objection, Your Honor! Gus Charnley isn't on trial here," he stated loudly, once again pointing to Rick. "Young Rick Heller is the one on trial."

"Objection sustained," said the judge. Rick wasn't sure what that meant, but he could tell by the consternation on Mr. Woodley's face that it wasn't good.

Margaret was the next one called to testify. As she took the stand Rick sat back, feeling relieved. He was sure things would go better with his mom on the stand.

"Animals live in captivity in zoos all over the world, Ms. Heller," said Mr. Price. "So why should this particular gorilla be in your cage instead of my client's cage?"

"Because Katie is different," answered Margaret tersely. "She can communicate! She can tell the difference between right and wrong!"

"So can my dog," said Mr. Price. "He knows it's wrong to go to the bathroom on the carpet."

"Your dog only knows what you've trained it to know," she corrected. "Katie can make moral decisions on her own."

"Can you prove that, Ms. Heller?" the lawyer scoffed.

"No," Margaret admitted. "My study was interrupted when Mr. Charnley took possession of Katie."

"So you have no concrete proof. Isn't that right, Ms. Heller?"

Margaret stared at the floor as she quietly answered, "Yes."

At noon they took a lunch break, but Rick was too upset to eat anything. So far the case was going badly. It looked as if Rick was going to lose and Gus would get Katie back. Rick cringed at the thought of her being locked inside that Plexiglas cage for the next thirty years.

When court resumed after lunch, Rick noticed that Lacey and her uncle Max hadn't returned. He figured they couldn't stand to watch the case go down the drain, so they'd split.

But Rick couldn't have been more wrong.

The courtroom doors suddenly burst open, interrupting the trial. Everyone turned around to see what the commotion was.

Katie was standing in the doorway! Uncle Max and Lacey were on either side of her, guiding her into the courtroom.

"Katie!" Rick called out, surprised.

Katie spotted Rick and broke away from Uncle Max and Lacey. She made a mad dash across the courtroom, barking wildly.

As she took a flying leap over several rows of seats, everyone scurried to get out of her way, in fear of the huge gorilla. Some people were fighting to get out through the courtroom door. Others threw themselves up against the wall or ducked under their seats. The whole place had been reduced to utter chaos.

The judge was banging her gavel, trying to quiet the courtroom. Unfortunately, no one could hear her over the yelling and screaming.

Katie jumped onto the defense table and fell into Rick's lap. She wrapped her long arms around him, hugging him with all her might. Mr. Woodley grabbed his briefcase full of papers and backed away from Katie in fear. He was looking like a total basket case at the moment.

"Katie miss Rick," the gorilla signed, then gave Rick a big, sloppy kiss on his face.

"Rick miss Katie," he signed back, wiping his face off.

Uncle Max and Lacey fought through the hysteria to get to the defense table.

"Why did you bring her here?" Rick demanded to know. "She's supposed to be in Canada!"

"Hey, it was her idea," Uncle Max said, pointing a finger at Katie.

Katie signed, "Me! Me! Me!"

"It was a *bad* idea! You should have stayed away!" Rick retorted. He looked over and saw a couple of court officers heading cautiously toward Katie. "Now the police can take her back! And they'll give her to Charnley again!"

The court officers approached Katie. Katie seemed to know they were coming to take her away from Rick, so she immediately let loose with a huge roar in their direction.

The court officers stopped in their tracks.

"Handling ferocious animals is definitely not in my job description," the first one gulped.

"Yep," the second one was quick to agree, "this is a job for Animal Regulation. Let them handle it."

"She's not an *it*," Lacey corrected them firmly. "She's a she!"

It wasn't until two Animal Regulation officers arrived with a harness and took Katie downstairs to a holding cell that order was regained in the courtroom.

Then the judge called a recess so she could have a private meeting with the lawyers in her chambers.

"I don't like my courtroom turned into a circus!" she lectured them with obvious displeasure.

"Your Honor," began Mr. Woodley, "I can assure you this came as a complete surprise to me too."

"I believe that," Mr. Price said with a smirk. "You should have seen the look on your face when that overgrown chimp jumped on your table!"

"Enough!" ordered the judge, glaring at the other lawyer.

"However, since she is here, the defense does have a request concerning Katie the gorilla, Your Honor," Mr. Woodley announced.

"And what might that be?" she asked.

Mr. Woodley swallowed nervously, then said, "We wish to put Katie on the stand. We'd like her to testify."

Mr. Price burst into laughter. "Yeah, that's a good one!"

The judge stared at Mr. Woodley in disbelief. She could tell he was serious.

"You want me to put a gorilla on the witness stand?"

"Yes," he answered.

"And who's going to question her?" asked the other lawyer mockingly. "Tarzan?"

Mr. Woodley ignored him. "Your Honor, it is an established fact that the gorilla has a working knowledge of sign language. We can have a sign language interpreter brought into the courtroom. He will sign the questions to Katie, and then interpret her responses."

Ed Price scoffed loudly. "This is the nuttiest thing I've ever heard, Your Honor."

"It is highly irregular," the judge conceded.

"Please, Your Honor," insisted Mr. Woodley. "Give her a chance to prove that she has a high level of intelligence and shouldn't be kept as an attraction at a flea market!"

Ed Price's smile quickly disappeared when he realized the judge was considering Mr. Woodley's request. "Hold on here," he said, his hands making a time-out signal. "The defense's motion is ridiculous. That dumb animal can't possibly add anything to this case that hasn't already been—"

The judge cut him off in midsentence. "Then you

shouldn't have any objection, should you?" she asked pointedly.

Ed Price was about to say something else, but the judge was already getting up and motioning them back into the courtroom.

"Your Honor, the defense would like to call its next witness."

Court was back in session. The courtroom was filled with an air of excitement, as everyone knew what was about to happen: a gorilla was going to take the stand.

The judge nodded at the defense table. "You may call your next witness," she stated, looking as if she hoped she wouldn't be sorry for allowing this.

"The defense calls Katie the gorilla to the stand."

Everyone sat forward in their seats, anticipating Katie's arrival. The side doors swung open and the two Animal Regulation officers led a very nervous Katie into the courtroom. She had a thick restraint harness around her chest with a long leash attached.

Rick saw how nervous she looked and leaned over to Mr. Woodley. "She's gonna freak," Rick whispered. "Crowds scare her!"

"We don't have a choice, Rick!" Mr. Woodley hissed back. "This is the only way to save her from Mr. Charnley."

Rick waved across the courtroom to get Katie's attention. She turned and hooted quietly at him.

Rick signed "Katie be good" to her, then held up something for her to see.

It was the drawing Rick had made on the beach, the

one of them watching the sunset together. Rick had colored it and added a lot of rich detail. It was now an excellent piece of artwork.

"Good," Katie signed from across the courtroom.

The Animal Regulation officers maneuvered Katie onto the witness stand, where she sat in the chair obligingly. Seated in front of her was a timid-looking man wearing thick-lensed glasses.

"Mr. Welch will be interpreting both the counsel's questions and the witness's responses," announced the judge, referring to the bespectacled man. Then she looked expectantly at Mr. Woodley. "You may begin."

Rick's lawyer got up and walked gingerly to the witness stand. Katie eyed him suspiciously.

"Your name, please?" asked Mr. Woodley.

The interpreter signed the question to Katie. Katie snarled at him. Mr. Woodley retreated a step.

"Come on," he urged gently. "Tell us your name."

The interpreter signed again. This time Katie threw her head back and let out an enormous, high-pitched scream.

Everyone in the courtroom braced themselves, ready to run for the door again. The Animal Regulation officers quickly moved in, yanking on Katie's leash to restrain her.

Rick dropped his head into his hands, unable to watch any more.

"Your name is Katie, isn't it?" Mr. Woodley said slowly, as if he were talking to a small child. "Isn't your name Katie?"

Ed Price stood up, exasperated. "Your Honor, this is going nowhere," he stated.

"I'm afraid I have to agree with that," replied the judge, shaking her head at Mr. Woodley. "This is going nowhere fast."

"Wait a minute!" Rick suddenly shouted. "I know how to calm her down!"

All eyes in the courtroom went to Rick as he started digging into his pocket. He pulled out a bag of M&M's.

"She loves these!" he exclaimed.

Katie recognized the bag immediately. Her eyes lit up and she hooted eagerly at Rick.

Rick took an M&M and flipped it at Katie. She saw it coming and effortlessly caught it in her mouth. That seemed to calm her down a bit.

"Now, will you tell us your name?" asked Mr. Woodley.

The interpreter signed the question to Katie. To everyone's amazement, Katie then signed back to him. The interpreter turned to the judge, clearly stunned.

"She said her name is Katie," he said in awe. "She . . . she really said it."

"Please continue with the questioning," the judge said, giving Mr. Woodley a smile.

The lawyer stepped closer to Katie, looking more confident.

"Do you know the difference between true and false, Katie?" he asked, then watched as the interpreter signed the question to her.

Katie thought for a moment, then signed back, "Yes."

107

Mr. Woodley then asked, "And will you promise to answer my questions truthfully?"

The interpreter signed the question, and then Katie signed her answer.

"She says, 'Katie good girl,'" reported the interpreter with a smile.

Mr. Woodley glanced around the courtroom. Everyone present was riveted to Katie's testimony.

"What does Katie love?" asked Mr. Woodley.

"Katie love Rick," said the interpreter, reading Katie's hand gestures. "Love hug Rick. Rick take good care of Katie."

"And what does Katie hate?" asked the lawyer.

The interpreter signed the question, then watched Katie sign back.

"Katie hate man that put Katie in prison," he said when Katie was done.

Mr. Woodley grabbed a photograph from the exhibit table and held it up. It was a picture of Gus's Plexiglas cage.

"Is this the prison?" he asked.

The interpreter signed. Katie was quick to sign back.

"Bad prison! Katie out. Out! Out!" the interpreter said.

Mr. Woodley grinned with pleasure. It was finally starting to look as if he might win this case.

"No further questions," he said smugly, returning to the defense table. Rick gave him a high five.

"Great job!" said Rick.

"Thanks to you," replied Mr. Woodley.

The judge glanced over at the prosecutor's table. "Your witness."

Mr. Price had a worried look on his face. He stood, but instead of questioning Katie, he approached the judge's bench.

"Your Honor, what we're seeing here is nothing more than a fancy parlor trick. This animal has obviously been trained to respond in certain ways, ways that are meant to play on our sympathies. It is not worthy of this court—"

"Your Honor!" interjected Mr. Woodley, cutting the other attorney off. "The prosecutor is giving a speech. This is supposed to be a cross-examination!"

"So it is," replied the judge, then turned to Ed Price. "Either cross-examine the witness or sit down."

"Very well," responded Mr. Price, tightening his lips. He walked over to Katie and stood right in her face, evidently hoping to annoy her into misbehaving. Katie merely sniffed him.

"Rick's mother claims you know the difference between right and wrong," Mr. Price told Katie. "Well, can you tell me, is it right to have rules?"

The interpreter signed the question to Katie. She thought a moment, than signed back to him.

"Rules good," said the interpreter.

"And is it bad to break rules?" asked Mr. Price.

The interpreter signed to Katie. She signed back.

"Bad. Trouble."

Mr. Price let out a tiny smile, as if he thought he had the gorilla right where he wanted her.

"Wasn't it bad for Rick to break the rules?" he asked Katie.

When the interpreter signed the question, Katie didn't

seem to know how to answer. She looked over to Rick, confused. He wished he could do something to help her, but she was on her own. She had to prove herself to the court.

"Was it right for Rick to steal? And run from the police? Wasn't that bad, Katie?" Mr. Price asked, his voice rising.

Again, Katie didn't appear to know what to say. Frustrated, she barked at Mr. Price. He quickly backed up a few steps.

"Answer the question!" Mr. Price demanded.

Katie was still for a moment. She seemed to be considering her answer. Then she signed to the interpreter.

"Katie not know right or wrong," the interpreter said.

There was a disappointed gasp in the courtroom. Rick hung his head, feeling awful.

"Aha!" Mr. Price exclaimed, turning to the judge. "She just admitted she doesn't know right or wrong!"

Katie signed something else to the interpreter.

"What's she saying?" asked the judge.

The interpreter seemed puzzled. "Katie *feels* right or wrong."

"What the heck does that mean?" spat Mr. Price.

Katie reached over to the exhibit table and picked up the photo of Gus's Plexiglas cage. Holding it up, she signed to the interpreter.

"This feels wrong," he said.

Katie then hooted at Rick, pointing to his drawing on the defense table. Rick held it up.

"That feels right," said the interpreter, reading Katie's gestures.

Rick blushed with embarrassment. Across the courtroom, Margaret was beaming with pride.

Mr. Price was speechless. He couldn't stop staring at Katie; he seemed totally amazed by what he had just witnessed.

"Mr. Price," called the judge, "do you have any more questions for Katie?"

Mr. Price just shook his head.

You could hear a pin drop when the judge came back into the courtroom, ready to deliver her verdict. Rick sat breathless, dying to know what was going to happen to Katie.

"Will the defendant please rise?" asked the judge.

Rick pulled himself to his feet and gritted his teeth.

"In the case of the state of California versus Richard Heller," she began, "I find the defendant guilty."

Rick's heart sank. Now he'd never see Katie again. The judge would send him back to juvenile hall and Katie would be locked in Gus's cage for the rest of her life. Rick felt like a total failure for letting Katie down.

But the judge wasn't finished yet.

"And I sentence Mr. Heller to one thousand hours of community service, working with Katie."

"What?" said Rick. He must have heard the judge wrong.

"Furthermore," the judge continued, "I am removing Katie from Mr. Charnley's custody and naming Richard Heller as her new legal guardian."

The courtroom exploded in cheers. Suddenly everyone was jumping up and screaming with joy. Everyone except Rick. He was too stunned to react.

Rick's lawyer leaned over and whispered, "Congratulations, son!"

Margaret raced over, embracing him. "You did it!" she squealed, beaming proudly.

Uncle Max was right behind her, patting Rick on the back. "Like I told you, never give up when you believe in something."

But Rick was too stunned to respond to any of them. None of this felt real to him. It was all too good to be true.

Lacey grabbed Rick and rewarded him with a big kiss, right on the lips! Rick felt a bolt of electricity shoot through his whole body. When the kiss ended, he was finally able to speak.

"Wow!" he shouted.

THIRTEEN

RICK HAD HAD NO IDEA HE COULD SEE GORILLAS in Hawaii. To him, Hawaii seemed like a place for great surfing, hula dancers, and lots and lots of beach parties. But gorillas? No way. He figured they could only be found in Africa.

But Hawaii, as it turned out, was the location of the Walden Animal Foundation. The foundation maintained a large preserve where rare and endangered animals could live in safety. Nestled deep in the dense woods of Maui, the enormous sanctuary looked just like the rain forest in Africa. It was a far cry from being locked inside any cage.

Jack Graham ran the place. He was a huge, burly man, and Rick couldn't help thinking he looked just like a grizzly bear. Jack presently had twelve gorillas living in the preserve. Two of them were still very young, about the same age Katie had been when she was stolen from Africa.

When the news of Rick's court case reached Jack, he had immediately invited Rick, Margaret, and Katie to visit the foundation. While there, they could attend a seminar that was being held on primate intelligence.

Katie, of course, would be the highlight of the seminar.

When they got to the beautiful island of Maui, Rick had no interest in surfing, hula dancers, or beach parties. He wanted to spend all of his time at the Walden Foundation.

Jack wanted to see how Katie would relate to other gorillas, so he set her loose in the preserve area. Jack and Rick then went inside the main building so they could watch her through a large observation window.

Katie romped through the jungle preserve with sheer joy. It was like she was free again! Free to run and play and jump and swing—with no cage to hold her back.

Katie then encountered the two baby gorillas. They acted shy and timid around her, probably because they didn't know Katie. She was a stranger to them.

Katie reached into a nearby tree and pulled down a couple of bananas. She offered each of the baby gorillas a banana as a peace offering. Then she signed to them, "Banana good."

The baby gorillas stared at her hand gestures in wonder. They had no idea what she was doing.

"Banana good," she signed patiently. "Banana good."

Totally in awe, Jack watched Katie signing to the young gorillas. "She is one smart girl."

"Yep," agreed Rick. "She's telling them that the bananas are good."

Katie continued signing "Banana good" to the young gorillas. They watched her, then tried to imitate her hand gestures. She was teaching them sign language!

"I wonder how she'd get along with the other gorillas," Jack mused aloud.

"Do the other gorillas all get along together?"

"Not always, no." Jack chuckled. "They're just like any other family. Sometimes they fight, but then they always make up, because they love each other. I guess that's what being a family is all about."

"Yeah," echoed Rick, deep in thought.

Margaret was asked to give several lectures about Katie. The lecture hall was crammed full of eager scientists when she spoke. Margaret told them about her two years of teaching and observing Katie. She even presented a slide show for the scientists, with pictures of Katie taken during her time in captivity.

Rick stood in the back of the auditorium watching his mom's slide show. He chuckled at a slide of a very young Katie playing with some building blocks. And a slide of Katie looking through her Viewmaster. And a slide of her asleep in her rubber tire.

Then Margaret showed some slides of Katie's chainlink cage in the lab. Rick's smile disappeared. Sure, it was a nice cage—a heck of a lot bigger and better than Gus Charnley's Plexiglas prison—but it was still just a cage. Rick's face darkened. He couldn't stand to watch any more of the slide show, and slipped out of the lecture hall.

That night he didn't sleep at all. He tossed and turned all night, wrestling with a tough decision.

"It's been great having you guys here," Jack was saying as he loaded Margaret and Rick's luggage into the back of his Jeep. "You and Katie were the hit of the seminar."

115

Margaret and Rick were standing with him near the edge of the jungle preserve. They were dressed to go to the airport.

"Thanks for having us, Jack," Margaret said with a warm smile.

"I sure hope you'll bring Katie back again," Jack said to Rick. "And your mom, too," he added shyly.

But Rick wasn't listening. He stood looking at the tiny cage that was sitting in the back of the Jeep. Katie was inside the cage, staring out the window at the preserve.

"Rick, let's go," called Margaret as she and Jack climbed into the Jeep. "We don't want to miss our plane."

Rick didn't get in. Instead, he opened the Jeep's tailgate, then snapped open the door on Katie's cage.

Rick signed to her, "Out. Katie out."

Katie looked at him questioningly, then scrambled out of the cage. She leapt out of the Jeep and into Rick's arms.

"What are you doing?" Margaret asked, confused.

Rick swallowed hard. "Mom . . . I want to leave Katie here."

Margaret looked as if she couldn't believe what she was hearing. "What . . . ? For how long?"

"Forever," he said. "For the rest of her life."

Margaret stared at her son in shock. "Are you sure?"

Rick nodded, then turned to Jack. "Is it okay with you, Mr. Graham?"

"Well, sure," replied Jack. "We'd be more than happy to keep her here."

116

Rick breathed deeply. Now came the hard part—telling Katie. He signed to her, "Katie be good gorilla. Stay here."

Katie shook her head, signing, "Katie stay Rick."

"I know you want to stay with me," he signed back. "But it's better for you here. This is where you belong, not in a cage."

Katie shook her head again. She signed, "No! Rick promise!"

"I know I promised," Rick signed, fighting back tears. "I promised I'd never leave you, but you have to go be a gorilla now. And I have to go be a kid."

Katie cocked her head, studying Rick's pained face. Then she looked over her shoulder at the wide expanse of jungle.

"Go," said Rick. It was barely a whisper.

Katie dashed toward the trees on all fours. In a flash she was eight feet up, swinging from branch to branch. She stopped, balanced on a limb, and looked back at Rick for a moment. Then she turned and disappeared into the trees.

Margaret put her hand on Rick's shoulder. Trembling, he spun around and hugged her tightly.

"I'm sorry, but I had to do it," he sobbed.

Margaret squeezed him more tightly. "Don't be sorry. You did what felt right. And it's what I should have done a long time ago."

Jack cleared his throat before saying, "We'll take good care of her, Rick. Don't worry."

Rick was too choked up to answer. Margaret gave Rick a kiss on the cheek, then led him back toward the Jeep.

"Let's go home, son," she said.

They climbed into the Jeep and Jack drove them down a winding dirt road that would take them out of the preserve. Pretty soon they'd be at the airport and heading back to California.

Rick sat numbly in the back seat of the Jeep. He looked over at the empty cage and saw Katie's Viewmaster lying there. It broke his heart. He grabbed it, clutching it tightly against his body.

All of a sudden, Rick noticed Katie running alongside the Jeep. She hooted, trying to get the Jeep to stop.

"Stop the Jeep!" Rick screamed.

Jack stepped on the brakes. As the Jeep screeched to a halt Rick threw open the door and jumped out. Katie ran toward him as fast as she could. When she finally caught up to him, she threw herself in his arms.

"You dad now?" she signed.

Rick was confused. "What does that mean?"

Katie signed, "You go away and never come back. Like dad."

Rick looked at her with a pained expression. "No," he signed with trembling hands. "I'll come back. I'll see you again, I promise. But this is your home now."

Katie studied Rick's tearstained face. She seemed to understand why she had to stay in the preserve and he had to go away.

"Eyes wet," she signed to him.

Rick nodded. "Yeah . . . eyes wet." There was no way to hide it from her this time.

Katie backed away a few steps, taking a good look at Rick.

"Love hug Rick," she signed.

Rick smiled through his tears. "Love hug Katie," he signed back.

They stood there a few more seconds, and then Rick couldn't bear it anymore. Bravely he turned away from Katie and walked back to the Jeep. He didn't look back.

The Jeep pulled away, leaving Katie behind in the vast jungle. She watched the Jeep getting smaller and smaller in the distance, and then it was gone. She was now alone in her new home.

Katie noticed a flock of birds circling overhead. Tilting her head back, she studied them curiously. They reminded her of the birds she had seen so long ago in Africa. As the flock flew over the trees, Katie started loping through the forest after them.

Pretty soon she was joined by the other gorillas. They ran alongside her, playfully hooting and barking at Katie. They were to become her new family.